PRAXIS
NOVELLAS

Susan,
I failed math so many
times at school I can't even
count.

:)

PRAXIS
NOVELLAS

MOSAIC CHRONICLES BOOK TWO

THE FOCUS ~ THE MANOR ~ THE ANGEL

ANDREA PEARSON

This is a work of fiction, and the views expressed herein are the sole responsibility of the author. Likewise, characters, places, and incidents are the product of author's imagination, and any resemblance to actual persons, living or dead, or actual events or locales, is entirely coincidental.

SERIES BY ANDREA PEARSON

Kilenya
Kilenya Romances
Kilenya Adventures
Mosaic Chronicles
Ranch City Academy

THE FOCUS

DEDICATION

To my mom, Betty
For being the best cellist I've ever known.

And to my older brother, Erik
Who's also pretty good. :-)

THE FOCUS

ℬ ✦ ℭ

Nicole lugged her suitcase and cello up a steep, narrow street in Hoglin, Ohio. She blew a strand of blond hair out of her face. Only ten more steps and she'd take a break.

Biting her lips, she heaved again, grunting with the effort and forcing the wheels of both cases—suit and cello—to grind against the cobblestone. She couldn't believe the stupid rental car wouldn't fit on the stupid street. Who had the dumb idea to build a street this cramped?

If she'd been able to Channel properly, she would've at least lifted her suitcase with wind, making it feel lighter.

At nine steps, she stopped. "Okay, call me a wimp," she whispered to herself, staring at the buildings surrounding her. Like the street, they'd been poorly built. In fact, most of them should have been condemned. They were coming apart, leaning over, with fallen bricks and shingles littering the ground around them.

At least the smell of the canal she'd been forced

to cross was fading. Brown, murky water that stunk of sewage and rotted fish—yuck.

Nicole pulled a slip of paper out of her jeans pocket. The address she looked for was seventeen Ginley Street. She looked up—the house closest to her was number eleven. She was a little more than halfway.

Taking in a deep breath of humid air, Nicole continued forward again, wishing the cases were lighter.

As she glanced at another house, she forgot about the steepness of the street and the heaviness of her suitcase. She couldn't believe she hadn't noticed the people earlier.

An older couple sat on a pair of rocking chairs at house twelve. She smiled at them, about to set down her case to wave when both glanced away and avoided further eye contact. Rude. The man next door doing yard work also refused to look at her.

Turning, she saw others—all acting the same. Older, not talking to each other, and definitely not looking at her. Nicole realized that at eighteen, she was the youngest person on that street by forty years at least. That wasn't very unusual, except for the fact that Misto University was nearby. Surely there were young couples living here, or students, at least?

After another ten minutes of heaving her things up the steep street, she arrived at number seventeen and paused to catch her breath while checking it out.

"How am I going to live here for three weeks?"

she whispered.

The edifice was tall, badly built of course, and okay, more sturdy than many of the other buildings on the street, but still! Her mother would have a cow if she saw it. "Good thing she won't." Nicole smiled.

Her parents were so proud they'd been able to have a fourth child—an Arete—which meant magic in the family. *Their* family! Imagine that! But she intimidated them, and they pretty much let her do whatever she wanted. After she'd graduated from high school and been accepted into Katon University, they'd maintained contact only through email and occasional cell phone conversations. Except for one visit by her mother . . . which Nicole would rather forget.

Nicole was fine with the arrangement. And anyway, she'd recently found out that the only reason they even had an Arete in the first place was to keep up with appearances.

Just then, the front door opened, interrupting Nicole's thoughts. An elderly black man with a thick head of white hair limped out. He approached her with caution, then rested on his cane. "Ms. Williams?"

"Yes?"

"I'm Mr. Landon, the building manager. Welcome." He bent over and, with some struggling, picked up her suitcase. She hesitated, watching him, but once he got it off the ground, he handled the large luggage just fine, maneuvering it into the building. He held the door open for her and she jumped to follow, pulling her cello along behind her.

Mr. Landon led her to an elevator, hit the up button, then turned away and stared out the front window while waiting. The expression on his face, while not unfriendly, showed he didn't want conversation.

Nicole fiddled with the strap on her cello case, wishing the elevator would hurry. It was stuck on floor three. Should she say something, maybe about the weather? Ask him about his family? No—many people considered that rude. But she did notice a wedding band on his left finger. Would it be safe to talk about his wife? She glanced around the lobby, looking for signs of a womanly presence. The decayed walls and old, eighties-style pictures didn't give her much information.

With a rattle, the elevator door opened. Mr. Landon entered, then held the door for her again and pushed the sixth button.

After a hard jolt, the elevator started rising. Nicole jumped into the corner, bracing herself against the sides. Wow! She was jumpy. A little giggle escaped from her mouth. She clamped a hand over her mouth, her face flushing. She was more embarrassed about the giggle than her reaction to the jolt.

Mr. Landon acted as if nothing had happened.

Finally, the thing came to a stop and the door rattled open. Nicole followed Mr. Landon down the hall to the right.

Outside room 602, he stopped, opened the door, and dragged the suitcase inside. He gave her the key, then left, pulling the door shut behind him.

Nicole stared at the thin piece of wood and flimsy lock that separated her from the rest of the building. Not very reassuring.

She took a deep breath and turned, deciding to explore. But what she saw definitely wouldn't take much time to investigate. The place was *small*. And maybe she was used to having a huge home—her parents were anything but poor—but the room in front of her was *tiny*. It could barely pass as an apartment.

The main room was made up of a kitchen and living area. An old TV—probably black and white—with an antenna faced an orange-and-green plaid couch. The kitchen was more of a kitchenette: a small, two-burner stove, barely existent sink, and a table with one chair. No counter.

Nicole opened the door on the right, revealing a bedroom half the size of her bedroom at Katon University, and a fourth the size of the one at home. Maybe even smaller than that. There was hardly enough space for a twin-sized bed and dresser, which were crammed in together. There were two doors to the right of the dresser—one for a closet with three shelves and the other for the bathroom, which, of course, was tiny, and had only a toilet and sink.

"Where's the shower?" Nicole asked herself. She felt panic rise up in the back of her throat. She couldn't possibly go three weeks—let alone a day—without showering!

She searched the entire apartment again. Which, of course, only took twenty seconds. With relief, she discovered a shower head above a drain in the corner of the kitchen. A shower curtain hung from the ceiling and swiveled around the head, allowing privacy. Nicole had assumed the curtain covered a window. Which it did. She'd have to be careful to keep the window covered while not splashing water all over the kitchen during her showers.

"This is ridiculous."

She sat on the edge of the couch and pulled her phone out of her purse.

Lizzie, her best friend, picked up on the first ring. "Hello? How are you? Did you finally get there? What's it like?"

Nicole smiled with relief at hearing Lizzie's familiar voice. "You'll never believe this place . . ."

℘ ✦ ℆

Nicole was awakened in the middle of the night by strange music drifting through the vent in the ceiling of her bedroom. The harmonies sounded off, the beat different from anything she'd ever played. It took her several moments to realize it was coming from a cello, which surprised her. She'd played the cello for years—she should be able to recognize it, regardless of how it sounded.

After identifying the instrument, she switched to guessing the composer. But after several moments, she gave up—the music was so off from what she'd heard before. She fell back asleep.

Nicole woke up early the next morning, eager for her first lesson with Professor Stephen Nielsen, a Wind Arete who used the cello as a medium. He was supposed to be one of the most powerful in the country.

As she was leaving, she ran into Mr. Landon and decided to ask him about the cellist from the night before.

"That's Mrs. Anna Morse, an old British woman. I hope she didn't disturb you. She chose the top floor because she likes playing late into the night and it's farthest from my office. Let me know if she causes too much of a distraction and I'll move you."

Nicole nodded and left, pulling her cello down the street. She crossed the canal and passed her rental car, deciding to walk and save the gas money. Besides, the weather was so nice! Seattle was beautiful in its own right, but she really missed seeing the sun regularly.

The stroll to campus took twenty-one minutes and, once she was past the smell of the canal, was refreshing. She was used to walking that far with her cello, and she daydreamed the entire way about a particular guy she'd started liking—and had even kissed—since moving to Seattle. His eyes, smile, laugh. How it would feel to have his arms around her again . . .

Austin had kissed her while on a Katon

University expedition to Arches, but he hadn't touched her since that day, except for holding her hand once. She chose not to dwell on that, though, remembering his promise to help her Channel when she got back from Ohio. They would have plenty of opportunities to kiss later. She hoped.

Thoughts of him left her when she got to campus. It was breathtaking. Late-blooming flowers lined the cobblestone walks. Ivy grew on the buildings. Tall, magnificent trees—so unlike the trees on campus in Seattle. Or even Texas, where she'd grown up. She had no idea what they were, but the bark appeared smooth and nearly free from blemishes.

Other students—a few of whom were Aretes—lounged on benches, studying from books or laptops.

After finding the correct classroom, Nicole explored the art and music building. Guided by the sound of music, she wandered down a long hallway and into an auditorium where a symphony was rehearsing. She sat in the back, wondering if any of her fellow students from high school were there. The piece was one of her favorites—Smetana's *Moldau*—and she closed her eyes, feeling herself pulled along with the rolls and flow of the song. The musicians were pretty good, actually.

Ten minutes later, the rehearsal ended and students filed from the auditorium. The conductor, a silver-haired gentleman, walked toward the top of the auditorium where Nicole sat, followed by a few violinists.

"Yes, yes, that's fine. We'll take it a bit faster next time."

Nicole thought she could see him roll his eyes as the violinists left. He spotted her and smiled. "Violinists. Rare to find one who isn't a diva."

Nicole grinned. She couldn't agree more.

The conductor stopped walking. "You aren't one, are you?"

"No, I play the cello."

"Nicole Williams?"

She started. "Yes?"

He laughed. "I'm Professor Nielsen. I believe you're here to study under me."

Nicole stood, extending her hand. "I am! Looking forward to it too." She motioned to the stage. "They sound really good."

He nodded. "Indeed they do. They're the best orchestra on campus and have worked hard. You won't be joining them, though, will you?"

She shook her head. "I'm just here for the three weeks."

"Ah, yes. But I've heard enough about you to know you could play with us if you had more time."

Nicole's cheeks flushed. "After what my parents put me through, I hope so." She glanced down at her cello. "Though, with the cello given to me by Katon University—long story behind that—I don't know if I could. This thing is pretty bad."

They laughed. Nicole was grateful—she'd get along well with him. Good thing too, since it was his job to help her further her expertise not only of the cello, but her special kind of magic.

He picked up a box of music at the back and she grabbed her cello, and they walked together to his classroom.

ဩ ◆ ℭ

An hour and a half later, Nicole left feeling discouraged and disappointed. They hadn't even discussed magic that entire block of time! He'd had her play practically everything she'd ever learned, and then gave her tons of sheet music to master before the next day. She sighed.

The early afternoon was chilly—the warmth of the morning had given way to possible thunderstorms, and Nicole walked quickly back to her apartment.

The one thing that had been different about Professor Nielsen from what she'd expected was his interest in the tenant living in her apartment—the one who played the cello. She'd told him about hearing the music, and how it had taken her several moments to figure out what instrument it was. He encouraged her to seek out Mrs. Morse and talk to her. Ask her where she'd learned cello and who was her composer.

જી • ભ્ર

After several days, Nicole discovered two things. First, Professor Nielsen probably wouldn't talk about magic for a while. He seemed determined to study music. Odd, considering he was a music professor. Nicole laughed to herself as she pulled the covers up to her chin one evening after a long day of practicing.

The second thing was how very difficult it was to find Mrs. Morse, and then even more difficult to corner her.

Every night since arriving, Nicole had stayed up late, listening to the foreign and strange music coming from above. Tonight was no different, and it was making her go crazy.

Leaning over, she dug through her purse and pulled out her cell.

She didn't even give her best friend time to adjust. "Lizzie, I have to figure this out!"

"Girl, why are you awake? It's got to be one thirty in the morning there!"

"It's driving me nuts—she plays all night long. I don't understand it. And it's with meaning. For a purpose. I need to know why!"

"Okay, honestly? I have to get up early. Just go talk to her—figure out what's going on. Isn't that what your professor told you to do?"

"Yeah, but she's kind of intimidating—she's really good. And I'm only eighteen. She's ancient. I saw her once. At least, I think it was her. She has to be in her eighties or nineties."

Lizzie snorted. "You? Intimidated? Come on." She took a breath. "You know, she might be able to help you with the cello itself, not just music. Approach her from that angle."

Nicole sat up in bed. "That's it! You're a genius!"

Lizzie chuckled. "I'm surprised—really surprised—that you didn't think of it yourself. Call me at a decent hour, after you've talked to her."

ℰℴ · ℭℛ

Two days later, Nicole was successful in that quest. They happened to be grocery shopping at the same time in a nearby store. When the store clerk called the stooped, little woman with the scarf over her head "Mrs. Morse," Nicole made her purchases and raced to catch up as the woman was leaving.

"Mrs. Morse?"

The elderly lady stopped and turned. "Mmm?"

"My name is Nicole Williams. I'm a cellist, and Mr. Landon said you also play the cello." Nicole smiled her most winning smile, and Mrs. Morse rewarded her with a grin that showed old, twisted teeth.

"Hello, dear," she said in a British accent. She continued walking.

Nicole kept pace easily. "I'm studying under Professor Stephen Nielsen at the university. But only for the next two weeks."

"How lovely."

And then, when Mrs. Morse realized she had a walking companion, she started chatting. A lot. Her dialect was so strong and so hard to follow, Nicole only caught a word here and there. She gathered that the woman had grown up in a small town somewhere near London. Or maybe far from London. Or maybe she grew up in London itself—Nicole had no idea. Her mind started to drift from the woman's monologue.

She couldn't help but wonder how Mrs. Morse still played the cello. Her fingers were bent out of shape, her shoulders stooped so much it had to be impossible to hold the instrument correctly. But hearing Mrs. Morse play, it was obvious she had been doing it forever. She'd probably adapted over the years as her body changed.

After several minutes of hiking up the steep road, they reached the apartment building. Mrs. Morse looked at Nicole with curiosity and asked a question that could only be something along the lines of whether Nicole lived there or not.

"Yes, this is my apartment."

They walked in together, Nicole holding the door for the elderly woman. Mr. Landon was at the front desk, typing at the computer. He ignored them as they waited for the elevator to drop to the first floor. Mrs. Morse continued chattering.

As they stepped onto the elevator, Nicole realized her opportunity was about to pass. She waited for a pause in Mrs. Morse's conversation, but one didn't come, so she put her hand on the woman's shoulder.

"May I ask a question?"

"Of course."

Nicole hesitated for a moment, trying to get up the courage. "I'd like to hear you play, and perhaps accompany you sometime."

The lady gasped and backed up against the elevator wall. All the blood rushed from her face, and her hands shook. She said something so quickly, Nicole felt a moment's panic at being unable to understand.

"I'm sorry—would you please repeat that?"

Mrs. Morse put a hand on her chest and took a deep breath. "I don't know . . . if that's . . . possible."

"But please, I'm learning to Channel my own powers, and I've heard you at night—you control things. I can sense it. It would help me so very much to learn from you."

Mrs. Morse shook her head and didn't say anything.

"You're so talented, and Professor Nielsen said I needed to talk to you and hear you play and actually play with you sometime. Please? I really, really need to understand how you do it."

Mrs. Morse finally nodded and said something that sounded like a positive answer, and Nicole couldn't help the smile that crossed her face. Her heart still raced, however, from the woman's initial response. Why would she freak out about having someone hear her?

The elderly woman got off the elevator on the seventh floor and beckoned Nicole to follow her down the hall. At the end, Mrs. Morse pulled out a set of keys and, with some concentration, got one of them into the lock on the door. She pushed it open and they entered a large, one-roomed apartment that was bigger than Nicole's place.

Nicole did her best not to look around, but couldn't help notice how sparsely furnished Mrs. Morse kept the apartment. Only a bed in one corner with a dresser near it. No decorations on the walls. No carpet or rugs—just scuffed-up floorboards and old linoleum under the kitchen sink.

Sheet music lay strewn across the floor near a music stand and Mrs. Morse's cello case.

After showing Nicole to a chair and waiting until she'd sat down, Mrs. Morse sat in another seat and pulled out her cello. She wiped down the front of it with a soft piece of cloth, a loving expression on her face, then tightened the bow. The cello was scuffed up and old looking—it had been well used.

Then she started playing. Nicole leaned forward, eager to see what the elderly woman did to bring the magic out through her cello.

But nothing special happened. Nicole recognized Mozart, Bach, and even some Beethoven, but nothing like what she'd been hearing every night. And even though Mrs. Morse was talented and the cello sounded and looked like an Amati, Nicole felt her heart drop.

After an hour at least, the woman played the last strain and lowered her bow. She didn't look at Nicole.

Nicole cleared her throat. "That was lovely. But . . . it's not like what I've heard you play. I want to learn from you—to understand how you captivate the magic with your cello. This is what I'm studying at Katon University—it's my magic. And it's why I'm here at this university, studying under Professor Nielsen."

Mrs. Morse didn't respond. She turned her face away, and Nicole frowned with confusion. Then something hit her—maybe the woman didn't know which songs Nicole meant. That couldn't be possible. She played them for several hours every single night—Nicole had dark circles under her eyes from staying up. Trying to remind Mrs. Morse of the tunes, Nicole whistled a few measures from one of the more prominent pieces.

Mrs. Morse jumped from her seat and crossed the space between herself and Nicole, surprisingly fast for a woman of her age.

"No! No, no, no!" she said, slicing her hands through the air in front of Nicole. "Not this. Not this!" She glanced at a large curtained window Nicole hadn't noticed earlier.

"What's wrong? The music is fascinating! It's very special and I like it!" Nicole stood and crossed to the window, intending to look out. But as she reached for the thick fabric, Mrs. Morse grabbed her hand and yanked her away. Nicole fell to the ground in shock, not even pulling her hand back from Mrs. Moore's grip.

The elderly woman tried to drag Nicole toward the door. She spoke very quickly, her thick accent masking the words.

With impatience, Nicole attempted to jerk her hand from the woman's strong grasp. "Let go! I'll leave now!"

Mrs. Morse's eyes widened and she released Nicole. It seemed like she realized what she'd been doing, and her shoulders slumped even more than they already were, a bright red flushing her papery cheeks. "Please," she said, motioning to Nicole's chair. "Please sit."

Nicole hesitated, unsure of what to do. Finally, she sat. She glanced at the door, wanting more than anything to disappear. Why would the woman respond like that? So violently? Nicole had never been treated that way. Where she'd grown up, people didn't try to throw each other around, especially practical strangers. And what was so bad about looking out the window? Nicole glanced that way and regretted doing so at once.

Mrs. Morse noticed and she started talking rapidly. Nicole shook her head—the woman could've been from Japan, for all Nicole understood.

The lady grabbed a pen and paper and scribbled on it for several long moments. She handed it to Nicole.

At first glance, the note wasn't written in English. But Nicole was able to pull a few words out here and there, and then finally, the overall meaning. According to the note, Mrs. Morse was begging Nicole's forgiveness. She'd been alone for too long and suffered from hysteria and episodes—Nicole wasn't sure about those two words—that affected how she treated other people. Then it mentioned being grateful for Nicole's apparent friendliness, that she hadn't met a young person in a long time.

Then the note said something that made Nicole's heart drop. How would she tell Professor Nielsen? Mrs. Morse was very sorry Nicole had heard her playing at night. She wasn't supposed to hear—no one was. It was Mrs. Morse's private time, and she wanted Nicole to relocate—buildings? Wasn't that a bit extreme? Nicole squinted, pulling the note closer. No, she must mean rooms. And Mrs. Morse would cover the difference in cost. Wow. Nicole glanced up.

Mrs. Morse looked like she was holding her breath—her entire body was tense, her face tight. Nicole couldn't believe the woman felt so strongly about *not* letting other people hear her play. For someone who'd been playing all her life, it was weird.

Nicole took a deep breath and slowly blew it out. "Well, if you feel that way . . ."

The expression on Mrs. Morse's face—still intense, but trying to hold back the hope that crept across her eyes—made Nicole feel bad about her harsh response earlier. Living like this would be so difficult. The woman was lonely and obviously scared of . . . practically nothing.

Nicole held back an urge to glance at the window. She pressed the note into Mrs. Morse's hand, looking into the woman's eyes. She tried to convey how she now felt—compassion for the woman's situation, willing to help wherever needed.

The woman needed a friend, that's what. And Nicole could be that friend. She'd volunteered in rest homes many times during high school, after all.

"I'll come visit you as often as I can while I'm here. I've only got two weeks left, but I'll make the most of it."

Mrs. Morse smiled uncertainly and showed Nicole to the door.

As Nicole walked down the hall to the elevator, she vowed to win the woman over. "All she needs is some Texas hospitality to cheer her up," she whispered to herself.

$$\wp \quad \bullet \quad \wp$$

The next day, after talking to Mr. Landon, Nicole moved two floors down. Apparently, Mrs. Morse had spoken with the building manager right after Nicole left and had paid the difference for the two weeks already.

Nicole was okay with the new arrangement— the apartment was much bigger than her first. The shower was located *in* the bathroom. She rolled her eyes at that and plopped on the bed, dialing Lizzie's number.

ℰ ✦ ℛ

Nicole soon discovered that Mrs. Morse wasn't nearly as approachable or happy to see her as the first time, even after frequent "music sessions" together. Along with her cello, Nicole almost always brought something with her: new music from Professor Nielsen, cookies—which Mrs. Morse loved—and sometimes Sudoku puzzles, another favorite of the woman's. It didn't seem to matter, however. Mrs. Morse got increasingly agitated about having Nicole in her apartment.

But Nicole was determined to win the elderly woman over. Being able to figure out why Nicole couldn't Channel was so important! Her future—her safety—depended on it.

Their visits always took place in the late afternoon, and no wonder—the lady played all night long. Nicole didn't understand how she functioned at all on the little sleep she got.

Nicole practiced her cello with the woman each time, but again, nothing exciting or different happened. Mrs. Morse would sometimes reach over and pencil in a note or circle a fermata or rest while Nicole played. And lessons with Professor Nielsen were similar. He still hadn't really brought up magic. This frustrated Nicole. She'd paid good money to come and study with him, and she usually left their lessons feeling dispirited. The latest he'd said was, "We first need to find the music you feel most strongly about. You have a great many passions—*The Moldau*, for instance—but they aren't pulling the magic from within."

Nicole didn't understand how she could be more passionate about music.

Lizzie was the only other person who knew of her obsession with Mrs. Morse's songs. Nicole wished she could talk to Austin about these sorts of things. She wished they could talk about *anything* at this point—just hearing his voice would almost be better than hearing Mrs. Morse play the cello. But they rarely communicated except through Lizzie.

"Nicole, this is seriously weird," Lizzie said. "There's something wrong with that woman, and something especially wrong with that apartment!"

"Professor Nielsen encourages it. He thinks it'll be the key to unlocking my magic."

"The *cello* is the key to unlocking your magic. Please, Nicole, stay away from that woman. Nothing good is going to come of this."

Nicole snorted. "Look, Lizzie, you're sounding worse than my dad. She's just an elderly woman who's protective of random things."

"And plays really creepy music late at night that she doesn't want other people to hear."

Nicole didn't answer—Lizzie was right.

"Okay, Nicole. Do what you want—you will anyway."

"Come on. Don't act like that."

"Like what? A friend? Trying to support you even when you get these crazy obsessions?"

"It isn't crazy."

"Whatever."

"Okay, I'm going to bed now." Nicole looked at the clock. Mrs. Morse would start playing soon.

"Right. You mean, you're going to listen from your old apartment now."

Nicole chuckled. "I'll call you tomorrow."

After they exchanged goodbyes, she hung up the phone, grabbed her jacket, and pulled on her shoes. She dashed to the elevator, punching the up button over and over again. "Come on, come on."

Lizzie was right—Nicole had started going back up to her old apartment and listening from there. Mr. Landon didn't lock the door, and she was able to sit on the bed right under the vent for as long as she liked. She kept the lights off, not wanting to draw attention to herself and her . . . okay, *weird* obsession.

A couple of nights, she freaked herself out, imagining that she wasn't alone in the apartment— that others listened with her. She did everything she could to keep thoughts like that away so she could tune in to the music.

Mrs. Morse was the most talented cellist she'd ever heard. No one like her existed or ever would. Her music was all over the place—harmonies so different and complex it was amazing there weren't two or three or even ten other cellos accompanying her. How did she play like that?

A few times, Nicole found herself wondering at her need to listen. Was it healthy?

Professor Nielsen believed it was okay, so she continued to do it.

Another thing—Mrs. Morse serenaded her window. Maybe unknowingly, but Nicole had seen where the woman's eyes drifted when she was involved in her playing.

One day, after seeing the elderly woman walk away from the building, Nicole sneaked upstairs. She wanted to touch Mrs. Morse's cello. Her senses heightened, realizing the woman could return at any moment, and she ran down the hall toward the room at the end.

She grasped the knob. It was locked. Nicole rattled the door—if she tried hard enough, she could probably break it down.

Then something moved at the other end of the hallway—a cat? A dog? Spooked, Nicole ran back to the elevator, hitting the button for her floor until the door shut.

She decided not to try again.

ℰ ✦ ℛ

"Nicole, you're an exceptional student. In the past two weeks, I've really seen this music come alive under your hand."

Nicole blinked a few times—it took several seconds for what Professor Nielsen had said to sink in. "Thanks."

He raised an eyebrow, and Nicole sighed. "Sorry, Professor. I'm just tired."

"Still listening to old Mrs. Morse?"

Nicole nodded. "And not learning anything new."

"Perhaps it's time you put a stop to it." He rushed to continue. "Not playing with her directly, but listening late at night."

Nicole looked down at the bow still in her hands. He was right. But listening was her favorite part. She hoped he wouldn't make her promise not to do it anymore.

"Besides," he continued, "I want to try something different today."

Nicole glanced up. He was sifting through a music book they'd gone over her first day under his tutelage.

"Ahhh, here it is." He folded the book backwards a couple of times so it would stay open, then placed it on the stand in front of her.

She stared at it, then looked up at him, trying to keep the distaste from her face. "*Pachelbel's Canon?*"

He chuckled. "Not exactly a cellist's favorite, I know, but it's not the music that's so important this time. I want to hear your magic."

She blinked. "Really?" Her heart sped up, and her palms started sweating. Finally! Magic! "Oh, I'd love that!"

He chuckled again. "I know, I know, it's about

time. I was hoping we'd Channel your powers through your favorite pieces, but this might just be the key."

"Bore me into magic, I get it. Funny." She lifted her bow, not even needing to check her fingers to know they were in the right place. She'd memorized the basic notes to this song years ago.

"Play just the first few measures."

She did so, without hesitation. Perhaps too quickly. When she'd finished, she waited to see what he'd say.

He steepled his fingers. "Okay. Do it again, but this time, focus on the air in this room. Try to move it—stir things up."

Nicole nodded, closed her eyes, and took a deep breath. She'd found that visualizing the wind as it rushed in and out of her lungs helped sometimes. She played the notes again, this time slower, with more purpose, concentrating, trying to find the ocean that separated her from her magic.

Nothing happened.

"It's just like always," she said, opening her eyes. "I know I'm a Wind Arete—"

"Of course you are; you hair is blond."

She nodded. "But magic just doesn't happen the way it should, if it happens at all." Unlike Lizzie, who'd made progress with her version of powers, and Austin, who wowed everyone with his abilities.

"We'll figure it out." He reached for the book, shutting it and putting it back on the shelf.

"Obviously, you don't need this in front of you. Try it again."

So she did. And this time, she quickly sensed the ocean of water and even felt the slight trickle of magic she'd sensed once before while playing.

"Excellent!" Professor Nielsen clapped. "I think we may have found a key here—music you aren't terribly passionate about, and it must be memorized and simple, allowing you to focus."

She gave him a half smile, trying to let him feel like he'd hit on something. But on the way home, the now-familiar discouragement hit her. She knew he was most likely right about two of the three things—she needed to have the music memorized, and it probably had to be simple, at least for now. But the other part just didn't sit right with her. How could she produce passionate magic without using passionate music?

℘ ♦ ℘

That night, she tried to convince herself not to do it. But her desire to sleep was nowhere near as strong as her need to hear Mrs. Morse play. So she sneaked upstairs. The night before, she'd decided that sitting in her old apartment wasn't close enough, and she'd gone to the seventh floor to sit right by the woman's door. This time, she brought a flashlight she'd purchased at the grocery store. She wanted to see each end of the hallway—way too spooky otherwise.

Mrs. Morse hadn't started playing yet. Nicole put her cell phone on silent and placed it next to her as she leaned against the wall near the doorframe. She looked up at the small, dangling bulb in the hallway—it gave off barely enough light, letting her see the area around her, but each end of the hall was dark.

Nicole flicked on the flashlight and shone it down the corridor, wanting to be sure she was alone. The night before, she'd only listened for ten minutes before chickening out and going back to her old room again. This time, she'd stay as long as possible. It wasn't like anything dangerous was going on in the apartment behind her.

The first smooth, graceful notes from the cello drifted through the wall. She smiled, leaned her head back, and closed her eyes.

After twenty minutes, Nicole noticed the music was different this time. Perhaps it was because she stayed longer, or maybe it was the close proximity. She startled when she heard something else coming from within the room—new patterns in the music. New sounds. Were there others playing with Mrs. Morse? Couldn't be—Nicole had never seen anyone enter or exit the room, aside from the elderly woman.

The wall behind Nicole thumped and she scampered away, crouching on the other side of the hall and staring at the spot. Low, guttural, bass thrummings and vibrations made the door tremble. Something *had* to be in there with Mrs. Morse!

Heart beating wildly, too scared to do anything else, Nicole turned the flashlight on again, shining it both ways. Alone still.

She cocked her head, listening to the new sounds and music drifting—sometimes rushing—from the cracks around the door. They sounded distant compared to the cello. Farther away. And definitely not originating from a cello.

Then something dawned on Nicole.

Mrs. Morse was a Wind Arete! She had to be channeling the sounds through her instrument, using magic to do so. It was the only explanation! Professor Nielsen had been right—Nicole really, truly needed to learn to play *just like Mrs. Morse*. She took a deep breath, her heart pounding hard against her ribs. A desire so intense she knew she'd never be able to ignore it flooded through her. She *would* play with Mrs. Morse at night.

ℰ ♦ ℬ

During her last week there, Nicole noticed a change in the woman's playing. It was more fervent, more stressed. There was a higher purpose to it, though Nicole still wasn't sure what. And any time Nicole saw the elderly woman, she looked even older than before—more stooped, with dark circles under her eyes, incredibly frail. Nicole's instincts to protect and mother were nearly unstoppable, but Mrs. Morse insisted she was just fine.

Four days before Nicole had to leave, Mrs.

Morse stopped admitting her to the apartment altogether. "Too busy too busy," was the only response Nicole got. She felt heart sick. She tried to convince herself it was because the woman was suffering.

But Nicole knew better.

One desire would not leave her alone. One desire consumed her dreams and every waking moment. It inhabited, haunted her. The need to play Mrs. Morse's music.

ℰ ✦ ℛ

The last day of class with Professor Nielsen arrived. Nicole was flying back to Katon University the following morning. With a heavy heart, she dragged herself to campus and his classroom.

She couldn't shake the feeling that the entire trip had been a waste. Professor Nielsen hadn't done anything for her at all. Sure, he'd instructed her and helped fine-tune her cello skills, but that wasn't why her teachers at Katon had sent her out to learn under him. He was supposed to find the one thing that would help her harness her powers. And he hadn't.

"Look, Nicole, we really have come far," he said after they'd gone over their notes of the last three weeks. His expression argued with his words, however. He seemed just as discouraged.

"I know, and I appreciate all you've done for me." Nicole closed her notebook, then took a deep breath. "I just never expected it to be so difficult."

"Many people never fully learn to Channel their magic. That isn't so rare."

She scowled, looking down at her hands. "Lizzie and Austin have no problem."

"And they're working with things more tangible—Lizzie uses fire, right?"

Nicole nodded.

"And Austin earth?"

She nodded again.

"You can see dirt and fire. You can't see wind unless there's something in it, marking its location."

"But Lizzie's power has to do with creating fire itself, and you can't see that until it's there."

Professor Nielsen got up to pace, then rested one arm on a shelf. "Yes, I know." He sighed, then rubbed his face. "I'm sorry—I can sense your disapproval about what we've discovered."

Nicole stood. "I don't want you to think you haven't helped me. You have! I know more about what I *can't* use than I did before. And sometimes the process of elimination is the only way to figure things out, right?"

Professor Nielsen half smiled. "Sure." He picked up his wallet from his desk and took out a business card. "This is my cell phone number—call me if and when you discover something. I might not have been as helpful as Professor Coolidge would've liked me to be, but I am quite possibly the only one who can help in the end."

Nicole understood what he meant. It wasn't arrogance—there were so many different ways a blond could use his or her power. Several Wind Aretes, like Nicole, used instruments. Of course, most of them were brass or wood instrumentalists, and understandably so. Professor Nielsen was the only advanced Arete who used the cello to produce wind magic. He was right—she had no one else to help her.

Unless . . .

"There's a chance Mrs. Morse's medium is also the cello."

He nodded. "I've thought of that, as you know."

"I'm going to listen to her one last time tonight."

He shook his head, smiling. "Yes, I suppose you will. Keep my card with you, though, just in case."

The two shook hands and said goodbye, and Nicole left campus. The walk back to the apartment building went by in a blur. After letting herself into her room, she made a snack before tackling the unwanted task of packing.

She finished right as the sun went down, and collapsed on the bed. Reaching with one hand, not wanting to get up, she grabbed the corner of her purse and pulled it toward herself, then took out her phone.

"Hey, Lizzie."

"Last night in Ohio, huh?"

"Yup."

Lizzie sighed. "Can't wait to see you again."

Nicole agreed, then they both fell silent for a moment.

"So," Lizzie said, "did Austin ever call you?"

Nicole's heart did a flip at the mention of his name. "No, and I'm not very happy about it."

"What? He didn't call even once during your whole entire time out there?"

"No . . ."

"He said he would. That idiot. He kisses you and then gets your number—yes, he did ask for it—and then never calls? He's so . . . dumb!"

Nicole smiled at Lizzie's indignation. "Don't forget that he's still hung up over his last girlfriend. Lizzie, I appreciate you trying to get us together, but if he's not interested, he's not interested. If he were, he would have forgotten the other chick and called me."

"I guess so. I don't get it—he said he *wanted* to talk to you." She growled. "He's too shy. It's so annoying."

Nicole didn't want to discuss him anymore. Too discouraging. "Can't believe I'm heading back tomorrow. Three weeks went by so fast."

"Was it worth it?"

"Not sure. I mean, Professor Nielsen's helped me become a better cellist, but what good is that without Channeling?"

"Oh, come on. You're only in your first semester of college. You've got years before you need to start worrying."

"I'm going to listen to Mrs. Morse one more time."

Lizzie fell silent, and Nicole knit her eyebrows. "You there?"

"Yeah. Nicole . . . I'm not sure that's a good idea."

"Why not?"

"Don't know. It just doesn't feel right. Please don't do it."

"You said the same thing two weeks ago and nothing happened."

"I know, but it's been different lately—it's dangerous."

Nicole snorted, rolling to a sitting position. "Right. Playing the cello is dangerous. Listening to someone *else* play the cello is even *more* dangerous."

"Don't be so flippant about this. You know something's going on."

Nicole didn't respond at first. "I have to do it." She took a deep breath. "Love you. I'll see you tomorrow."

"Wait, Nicole—"

But Nicole didn't hear what else Lizzie had to say. She hung up and lowered the phone, listening hard to something from upstairs. "She started," Nicole whispered.

Nicole left her phone on the bed and scrambled to find her flashlight. Without caring if anyone heard her, she rushed out of the apartment and up the stairs—the elevator was too slow and she didn't want to miss anything.

She was right. Mrs. Morse had already started playing, and at least ten minutes early. Already, the music sounded crazy and intense. Nicole paced outside the door, too nervous to sit, wishing she could help the woman with whatever she was doing.

The vibrations grew and grew until the entire building felt like it would fall apart. Nicole braced herself against the wall. The vibrations subsided, but the notes from the cello accelerated, coming faster, becoming more complex, and impossible to ignore. How was Mrs. Morse doing it? How were her fingers keeping up?

The woman needed help.

Nicole dashed to her apartment, grabbed her cello, and in less than two minutes was back at Mrs. Morse's door, knocking as hard as she could.

"Mrs. Morse? It's me—Nicole! Are you all right? Can I come in?"

The music stopped. Nicole heard a window bang shut and heavy curtains falling into place. All other sounds in the room dissipated.

Then the door opened and Mrs. Morse rushed into the hallway, tears pouring down her face. She flung her arms around Nicole, holding her tight, face pressed against Nicole's shoulder. She blubbered on and on, totally incomprehensible.

Nicole patted the woman's back. "It's all right. I'm here now." She bit her lip, unsure what to do or how to handle the sudden change in the woman who'd shunned her for the past several days. So she motioned to the cello she still held.

At the sight of it, Mrs. Morse nearly fainted with relief. She put her face in her hands and sobbed for a moment, then clutched Nicole's arm and pulled her into the room.

As soon as Nicole stepped across the threshold, Mrs. Morse calmed. She put her hand on her chest, took several deep breaths, then gave Nicole a weak smile. The woman ushered Nicole to a chair and puttered around the kitchenette, producing cups of herbal tea, one of which Nicole accepted gratefully.

The old lady sat in her chair, near where her cello and bow had been laid carelessly, her tea held tightly—forgotten—in her hand.

Neither said anything for a moment. Nicole sipped from her cup, half expecting Mrs. Morse to ask her to leave at any minute. The woman didn't. She sat with her body facing away from the window, but her left ear turned toward it.

Every now and then, the woman tensed, every visible muscle straining, her face white. Then she'd relax. This repeated over and over again.

After a while, Nicole couldn't stand it anymore. Someone had to do something about the situation. "Do you want me to see if the window is shut?"

An expression of horror crossed the elderly woman's face. "Oh, no, no, no." She babbled for several moments, using her hands to express herself, nearly spilling her tea. But when it was apparent that Nicole couldn't understand anything she said, she motioned for Nicole to wait. With some effort, Mrs. Morse lifted her frail body from the chair and crossed to the table where her pen and paper sat, along with several lit candles, adding their light to the hanging bulb above.

She wrote something brief and handed over the note.

Nicole squinted, trying to make out what was written. Again, it was an unfamiliar form of English, and it took several repeat reads to guess what the woman was trying to say. Mrs. Morse wanted Nicole to wait for a moment while she wrote a full account of what had been happening—why she played the cello at night and wouldn't let anyone listen.

Nicole looked up and nodded. "Yes. Please, go ahead. I'll stay as long as necessary."

Mrs. Morse grabbed a stack of paper and a pen, and started writing furiously. Nicole frowned. Would she even be able to read it?

Page after page fell to the side as Mrs. Morse continued her narrative. Nicole watched the expressions and emotions fly across the elderly woman's face as she experienced again what she wrote.

The papers piled higher, and Nicole started to wonder if there ever would be an end to the story. The only sound in the room was the scratching of the pen.

An hour later at least, Mrs. Morse stopped, frozen, eyes staring unseeingly, pen above the page. Her lips parted and an exclamation escaped. Dread crossed her face. She turned and looked at the curtained window behind her. Her hands trembled, and a massive shudder crossed her shoulders.

Nicole frowned, cocking her head, trying to figure out what Mrs. Morse had heard.

And then she thought she also heard it. Was it her imagination? A sound she'd never encountered before. Nothing terrifying about it—not horrible, just different. Low and musical. Did it come from a neighboring apartment building? It had to—it sounded distant.

Nicole shrugged it off, but the sound increased. Mrs. Morse completely freaked out.

She dropped the pen. It fell to the wooden floor with a clatter and she sprang from her chair. She grabbed her cello and bow, barely sitting straight enough to hold them correctly, and started to play.

The music wasn't anything like what Nicole had been listening to, and Mrs. Morse played more feverishly than Nicole thought possible.

Bow hairs started shredding. Mrs. Morse continued, staring at the window. Several moments later, a string broke. The woman didn't even pause, she simply adjusted her fingering to make up for the loss.

Nicole had been so intent on Mrs. Morse's playing that she hadn't looked at the woman's face yet. She did so then and gasped, a hand fluttering to her mouth. The sight was enough to make her wish she hadn't come.

The woman's eyes were so wide, they almost

popped from their sockets. Her usual pale face was blue from lack of blood. Her neck was so tense, the veins and muscle fibers beneath the taut skin were noticeable.

Mrs. Morse was absolutely and completely terrified.

Nicole jumped to her feet, wanting to run away, but unable to leave the woman like that. "What's going on?"

Mrs. Morse didn't respond.

"Please, tell me! Please tell me so I know how to help!"

Again, no response.

Nicole whirled, remembering she'd brought her cello. She pulled it up, rushing to tighten the bow, and quickly as she could, matched the tune Mrs. Morse was playing. Gratitude for the many teachers who'd taught her to play by ear flitted through her brain until she became encompassed by the music.

Louder and louder they played, even more wild than Nicole imagined. Mrs. Morse focused on the window. Perspiration dripped from her nose.

The window rattled, startling Nicole. The glass banged hard against the frame. Something was out there—something that desperately wanted to enter the room. And then Nicole thought she understood— Mrs. Morse played to keep that thing from entering. Or she played to appease it, or to make it stronger. Nicole didn't know which was the case, but Mrs. Morse needed help.

Nicole focused all her energy on following

the woman's example. She played, matching the harmonies and melodies. All her training and expertise came together as her fingers and bow flew across the strings. She concentrated on her breath as it rushed in and out of her lungs, trying to harness her powers. "Come on, come on!" But nothing happened.

Was the playing making the thing outside the window get stronger? Nicole pushed that thought aside—her gut told her whatever was there would gain strength regardless. Howling wind outside picked up and shrieked at the pane. The glass shuddered and the curtains billowed away as a slight breeze forced its way into the room through the cracks around the edges.

Then the glass burst and the curtains flew away, revealing a black, gaping hole. Nicole screamed. She looked to Mrs. Morse for help, but the elderly woman showed no sign of recognition that anything happened.

A fierce gale tore into the room and the sheets of paper from the desk flew through the air, scattering across the floor. The candles went out, and the light hanging from the ceiling started swaying. "Please, please don't break," Nicole said to the light bulb, not pausing.

The music coming from Anna Morse's cello picked up speed, if at all possible, and was more frenzied than ever before. Nicole slowed, panting. She couldn't keep up—she could no longer replicate the sounds on her own cello. Strong disappointment hit her in the chest. She hadn't summoned magic. Nothing had come to her—she hadn't been helping Mrs. Morse. Did she make things worse?

An even stronger gust of wind ripped into the room, forming a vortex that swirled around and around. The papers containing Mrs. Morse's precious account were lifted. They rushed faster and faster, joining the whirlpool of wind.

Nicole dropped her cello and bow, jumping for the sheets, trying to catch them. "No, no!" She caught hold of a paper, but it ripped from her hand, leaving a small piece behind which she thrust into her pocket.

Then the vortex gushed out through the broken frame. Nicole lunged for the papers, falling to the floor six feet from the window. She almost started bawling when she realized she'd lost everything—she'd never know what Mrs. Morse had written.

A sudden desire to look out that window pulsed through her system, so intense she couldn't ignore it, and she got to her knees. Music filled the air around her, coming from both inside *and* out. Something urged her to get to her feet and cross to the window, even while her heart screamed at her to run from the room.

She stood and took a haltering step forward. One more step and she was close enough to see what was on the other side. She looked, expecting the city lights below and the buildings of the university.

But there was no city. No lights.

Only blackness. A completely incomprehensible

void.

And shadows—shadows moving through that void.

Nicole felt her breath escape in a rush. The darkness was so near, she felt she could reach out and touch it. The shadows moved closer.

And then a bright yellow eye appeared. Just one. Followed by another. Then three more. Then four. Then a sea of yellow eyes blinked into visibility, all trained on her. The shadows inched forward.

A huge gust of wind rushed around her, whipping her hair into her eyes and mouth, taking her breath away. With a pop, the ceiling light behind her burst, thrusting her into full blackness. She was alone, aside from yellow spots and an unseeing old woman still playing a cello.

Nicole fell back from the window, gasping, wiping the hair out of her face. And then something occurred to her. Mrs. Morse *wasn't* a Wind Arete.

But Nicole *was*. And her magic *did* come through the cello—but not hers. The understanding of this fact filled her soul and she jumped back, following the sounds of Anna Morse's playing, tripping over her chair.

"Mrs. Morse! Mrs. Morse, give me your cello!"

The elderly woman didn't respond.

Putting her hands out, Nicole shuffled toward the woman on her knees. Avoiding being struck by the flying arm and fingers, she pried Mrs. Morse from the instrument and bow, ignoring as the woman fell to the ground. For a terrible moment, silence filled the room.

Nicole sat on the chair and yanked the cello into position. The moment it rested against her, with her left hand in the correct place, she felt a warmth spread from her chest and up into the middle of her skull. It was unlike anything she'd ever felt before.

Not taking time to consider what had happened, she started playing. She began with the first thing that popped into her mind—Pachelbel's *Canon*. But nothing happened. She didn't know what *should* happen. Maybe Mrs. Morse's tunes from earlier would do it? Nicole began playing those, leaning forward, staring at the black space.

She felt something stir in her heart, and lights began swirling around inside the cello, popping out through the holes on either side of the bridge. Magic! She couldn't tear her eyes from the void in front of her, but she knew it wasn't strong enough—she needed to try something else.

Just then, something happened that made her breath choke in her throat. One of the yellow eyes, at least a foot across, appeared in the window. Shadows—discernible, even in the complete blackness—spread out from either side of the eye, reaching in, creeping along the walls, ceiling, and floor. An ancient, magical pulse, originating from the eye, washed over her.

Nicole shrieked, nearly lifting her feet from the ground so the shadows couldn't touch her. She cast her mind everywhere she could think to put it.

Music! She needed something stronger than Mrs. Morse's songs!

Smetana's *Moldau* flew from her fingers, her bow following, and she started at the only part she could remember—somewhere close to the beginning when the cellos play a fast, river-like background harmony.

The lights sparking from her cello got brighter and brighter until they were no longer sparks, but flowing, flooding, illuminated air. A great dam burst around her, releasing the magic that had been pent up for so long.

The great eye blinked, trembled. The shadows stopped advancing.

Nicole played faster and stronger, concentrating as hard as possible. She moved onto other pieces she was just as passionate about. Songs by Schuman and Tchaikovsky. She chose composers of the Romantic era—all her favorites. The music she loved most.

And the lights and air rushed from the cello, bursting where Nicole directed them—toward the large creature blocking the window.

She wasn't sure, but it looked like the monster stepped away. Just a little. And then again.

But she realized something. She couldn't possibly stop this thing and the other forces trying to get into the room. The magical pulse was stronger now—these creatures were much more powerful than she.

Perhaps she could delay them long enough to get Mrs. Morse to safety. Maybe. She focused her energy through the music of the cello, directing the wind toward the unblinking eye. A sudden homesickness swept through her and she wished Lizzie was there with her, helping to make things right again. Nicole had no idea what she was doing.

Exhaustion—complete and utter—enveloped her, and she felt her limbs and joints try to freeze up. But still she continued, relentless. As she watched, the shadows dissipated. The eye moved until it was at least ten feet away.

She ran out of songs and started back at the beginning, with *The Moldau*.

Then the eye disappeared just as her body gave up. She could play no more.

Nicole dropped the cello. "Mrs. Morse?" No response. She felt around in the darkness until she found the woman and checked for a pulse. It was faint, and Nicole might have imagined it.

Not even caring that she was leaving behind an instrument that was worth several hundred thousand dollars—perhaps millions—Nicole grabbed Mrs. Morse and heaved her toward safety—a faint light from the hallway guiding her, shining underneath the door.

No telling how much time she had before the creatures returned—if they'd even left.

Nicole pulled Mrs. Morse from the room— luckily, the frail woman weighed hardly anything. She slammed the door behind them, then picked up the lady as best she could and stumbled down the hall, toward the elevator, praying it would come fast. No way could she take the stairs with a half-dead woman.

A low, guttural, musical note sounded behind her—muted by the door. Mrs. Morse cried out, making Nicole squeal with fright. The woman struggled to get away, but Nicole was stronger.

The entire building shook and Mrs. Morse fainted. Nicole braced herself against the wall. The elevator door opened and she stepped in, pulling Mrs. Morse with her. She punched the button for her floor over and over again, willing the doors to shut. They finally did. With a jolt, the contraption moved down, lower and lower, carrying the women farther away from the creatures on the seventh floor.

Nicole half dragged, half carried Mrs. Morse to her apartment. One of her neighbors opened his door and watched as Nicole dragged the lady past. He didn't do anything to help. The music from above increased and he cocked his head, apparently listening to it. He hummed along for a couple of measures, then smiled at Nicole and slowly shut his door. She almost dropped the old woman in shock. Why would he do that?

Nicole pushed into her room and put the lady on the couch. She ran into the bedroom, pulling out Professor Nielsen's business card and grabbing her cell phone.

"Professor? It's Nicole—sorry I'm calling so late."

"I'm awake—I had a feeling you'd be getting in touch."

Nicole explained to him what had happened—how she'd played her cello with Mrs. Morse, how the window had shattered and she'd seen eyes. She was about to continue when he interrupted her.

"You *must* get out of that building as soon as possible. Leave the woman and anything else that doesn't belong to you."

"I couldn't do that! She'll die! Those things want her!"

"Exactly! Nicole, please, listen to me. Whatever forces Mrs. Morse has been fighting know her—they'll follow wherever you take her. Leave her there and get out now!"

Nicole took a deep breath. "Okay. Where do I go?"

"Meet me outside my building on campus. My wife and I will be there in ten minutes."

Nicole grabbed her keys, phone, purse, and suitcase. She hesitated when she saw the cello case, but knew she couldn't risk going upstairs to get either instrument. After a cursory glance over the apartment, she left Mrs. Morse—still in a faint—on the couch and shut the door.

Luckily, the elevator was still on her floor. While waiting for it to reach its destination, she pulled the key to her apartment off the chain and dropped it. Mr. Landon would find it there.

She got off the elevator.

The building rumbled, pictures fell to the floor with a crash, and that low, musical note flooded around Nicole, forcing into her mind memories of the beasts she'd encountered while in Arches National Park. She panicked, realizing the creature had probably broken its way into Mrs. Morse's room.

Nicole raced through the front doors, not bothering to shut them behind her. Her arms were sore from playing, but she ignored the pain, holding her large suitcase to her chest. It didn't seem so heavy as last time, or perhaps her terror gave her strength.

Guided by the moon, she dashed down the steep road, almost tripping several times. The ground beneath her trembled. She didn't look back. Shadows flitted on either side of her.

Suddenly, something or someone grabbed her, nearly causing her to fall.

"Don't go—please don't go," an elderly man said.

A woman behind him also reached for Nicole. "Yes—you could get used to it." A smile lingered behind her words. Her pale eyes glinted in the moonlight.

Several others approached, exiting the buildings on either side of the road, all reaching for Nicole, grinning, eyes flashing.

The guttural, musical sound from the building increased and Nicole dropped her suitcase, clamping her hands over her ears. She watched the others, but they just grinned wider at her reaction.

The old lady nearest Nicole snatched her hands away from her head. "Enjoy it!" Her fingers pinched Nicole's wrists, and another woman grabbed

Nicole's shoulders, holding her in place.

"And girlie, you'll love what comes next!"

Nicole struggled against them, fighting their strong grips. She shoved and kicked and whirled, trying to get away. A sob escaped her throat. "Let me go! Please, let me go!"

The smells of the canal grew stronger, nearly suffocating her; the people didn't seem to notice.

With one final burst, punching and scratching and elbowing, Nicole thrust herself away. Leaving her suitcase behind, she raced forward, barely noticing she still had her purse.

She reached the canal and ran across the bridge. The people didn't follow—they stood on the other side, howling, begging her to return.

Her car doors were already unlocked—she didn't remember them being that way, but didn't care. She hopped in, tossing her purse on the seat beside her, and shut the door. She revved the engine and peeled away, driving as fast as she could to Misto University.

§ᴆ ✦ ᴄ§

By the time Nicole arrived at the university, her breathing and heartbeat had almost returned to normal. The lights on campus were cheerful—twinkling, reassuring. She parked in the lot nearest the music and art building and turned off the car, leaving her hands on the steering wheel. She'd made it. She'd actually made it.

After a moment of deep breathing, Nicole grabbed her purse and opened the door.

Professor Nielsen waved from the entrance to the building, a woman at his side, and Nicole walked toward them, a smile of relief spreading across her face.

છ૭ ✦ ભ

"I thought you said you'd be able to find it." Austin pocketed his phone and looked at Nicole.

She held her breath as his warm brown eyes stared into hers, but then pushed the twitter-pated feeling aside when what he'd said entered her brain.

"I can." Nicole turned to Lizzie, exasperated that she and Austin might not believe the street had existed. "Come on, you talked to me on the phone several times while I was here and heard all of my descriptions. It's not like I'd forget, especially after everything that happened."

Lizzie nodded, her red curls bouncing. "Yup. And you said it was a twenty minute walk from the university, right? But in which direction?"

Nicole didn't answer. How could an entire city street vanish? She turned back to the dirty canal they'd been following for the past forty minutes, trying to see something—anything. The smell of the murky water, along with the memories that accompanied that stench, made her gag. She pushed her thoughts away, focusing on the other side of the canal. Nothing popped out at her, and she growled in frustration.

The other two followed, Austin keeping up easily—he was several inches taller than Nicole's five-foot ten—but Lizzie, who was super short, had to jog to stay even with the others.

Lizzie and Austin had taken a weekend off from school in Seattle just so Nicole could show them the creepy place where she'd lived for three weeks. Three entire weeks! Finding the street—one that crossed this canal—shouldn't have been so difficult.

She growled again, refusing to believe she was going crazy, and faced the others. "Well, it was around here somewhere. Sorry I wasted the trip." She felt especially bad since she didn't know Austin very well—they'd only met a couple of months earlier. And even though he was friendly now and even a little flirty, she still felt him hesitating where she was concerned and it made her self-conscious.

"Not wasted," Austin said with an uncharacteristic grin. He so rarely smiled. "I'd always wanted to visit Misto University. It was fascinating—I could feel its ancient, magical pulse. It's no wonder so many Silvers are attracted to the area."

Nicole rolled her eyes at the mention of "Silvers," a nickname given to magical people when they got older. Elderly people deserved respect, not nicknames. "Yeah, the magic here is different from what we have back home, that's for sure." She didn't think Ohio was better than their campus in

Seattle. Different, yes, but not better.

Lizzie grabbed Nicole's arm, turning her away from the canal. "Seriously, can we go find food now? I'm starving."

"Sure . . ." Nicole sent one last searching look at the buildings and houses across the water, then followed Austin and Lizzie back to the rental car.

"Did Professor Nielsen ever wonder if you were telling the truth?" Lizzie asked after they'd settled into a booth at a pizza parlor.

Nicole shook her head. "Nope. The only thing we talked about was how Mrs. Morse's cello allowed me to direct my magic, while my own didn't." She glanced at Austin who seemed to want to say something. "What do you think?"

"I have theories," he said. "I think the cello has to be authentic—not a cheap knock off you could buy from eBay. It has to be an actual Stradivarius or made by someone equally talented of the past. Not only that, but an older instrument would better carry your magic, since the wood vibrates better than a new one."

Nicole nodded, sipping her water. It didn't surprise her how much Austin knew. He was smart that way. "Professor Nielsen said the same thing. Unfortunately, cellos like that are hard to find. And expensive."

Lizzie snorted. "Just call your dad and tell him to take care of it."

"No—I don't want to involve my parents. It would be best if I found it myself."

She sighed, wondering how she'd come up with the necessary money. "I still can't believe the street disappeared."

Austin watched her for a moment, then rubbed his chin. "Have you considered that maybe you're not meant to find it again?"

Nicole looked into his searching eyes, nearly forgetting herself there. She blinked, giving herself a mental shake. "I have, but I don't like it."

Lizzie chuckled. "Sounds like you're going to have to get used to the idea."

"Yes, most likely I will."

Nicole put a hand to her pocket, checking that the sliver of paper was still there. She couldn't make out the bit that Mrs. Morse had written on it, but at least she had it as proof that the night had really happened.

THE MANOR

DEDICATION

To my brother Glenn
Whose beautiful photographs practically come alive

THE MANOR

ℬ ✦ ℭ

Savoring the smell of chicken-flavored ramen noodles, Austin turned off the stove and dumped the noodles into a large bowl. He set the bowl on the counter to cool next to that morning's mail and opened a package he'd gotten from his older brother. Inside, he found a scrap of paper with scraggly writing on it taped over a framed 8X10 picture.

Austin,
Bought this for $150. Thought you'd appreciate it.
Call it a late eighteenth birthday present.
- Cody

Austin pulled the note off the picture and frowned. The image of a Victorian-styled manor greeted him, surrounded by trees and a big front lawn. It looked like one of many similar places dotting the city of Seattle, where he attended Katon University. And not only was the photograph—probably taken in the late

1800s—generic, but it wasn't very good. Definitely the work of an amateur, and not worth the price. Why would Cody pay so much for *this*?

Austin snorted at his older brother's obvious impulse purchase. He looked at the frame—a simple, $10 "steal" from Walmart, probably. He turned it over. The paper label on the back was partially ripped off. Only the right half remained.

nell Manor, Seattle.

"Nell" looked like it was the end of a word. But what word? He pushed the thought aside. This wasn't worth his brain power when he had food to eat.

Austin put the picture on the counter, grabbed his ramen noodles, then sat in front of the TV. He took a huge bite of noodles and turned on the system, searching for a documentary. While waiting for it to load, he called his brother, not bothering to identify himself when Cody answered.

"What's with the picture? They ripped you off."

Cody laughed. "Just wait—it's pretty awesome. The guy I bought it from had it for years in a box in his warehouse. I figured since you're a magical student and you're in Seattle where the house is, you'd figure out what's going on better than I could."

"*Arete* student."

"Whatever. Something only the fourth child of a family would understand." Cody chuckled again, then jumped into a discussion about the woes of university life at a school where there weren't many Aretes. "Dude, you'd never believe how *boring* it is!"

A few minutes later, they finished the conversation and Austin scarfed down the rest of his noodles. He grabbed his jacket, then left for study group. Midterms were about to happen, and though the material for Earth Arete was easy enough, he wanted to make sure he hadn't missed anything.

When he got to the class, his roommate waved at him from the front row. Austin hesitated. He looked at the back longingly, where he'd have fewer eyes on him, but joined Nate anyway. He scooted down in his seat, feeling his cheeks flush when the girl conducting the session smiled at him.

She promptly started the review. They discussed terms specific to their type of magic, including the different kinds of sand and dirt, and how to work with their strengths and weaknesses—stuff Austin had learned over a year before.

"Hey," Nate whispered an hour later. He looked paler than usual, his eyes red. "This is way over my head, and you're obviously bored. Let's go home and watch a movie."

Austin breathed a sigh of relief, grabbed his things, and they quickly left the room. The sun had set during the session, and he pulled his jacket closer around him. He'd never get used to the chilly, humid Seattle weather. Montana was much drier—and warmer at this time of year.

They flicked on the apartment lights, then Austin set up the system while Nate rummaged through cupboards, most likely looking for junk food.

"So . . ." Nate said.

Austin waited, rolling his eyes. Nate's tone of

voice suggested a conversation Austin probably didn't want to have.

"Uh . . ." Nate continued. "Okay. I'm just going to ask it. Are you into Lizzie?"

Lizzie? Short, hyper, funny Lizzie? Had Austin done something to make Nate think he liked her that way? And if so, did *she* think it too? That would be really awkward. "No, man. She's a good friend, but she's not really my type."

"What *is* your type?"

Austin shrugged, flipping through the DVD collection. He wasn't about to answer. Their friendship was the type that wouldn't last after graduation, and definitely not the type where Austin would feel comfortable spilling his guts. Besides, Nate had met Savannah—the girl Austin dated in high school—plenty of times. He already knew Austin's type.

Deciding the DVDs needed a more thorough inspection, he took the black leather holders from the shelf and plopped on the couch, starting from the beginning. "You about ready?"

"Just getting the cheese dip warmed up."

"What movie do you want to watch?"

Austin heard the microwave beep.

"Don't know." Nate paused. "Why do you have a picture of an old house?"

Austin flipped to the James Bond movies. He owned every single one of them—originals and the more recent. "Ugly, isn't it? My brother spent $150 on it. Not worth it."

"It's not all bad, but yeah, definitely not a steal."

"You're from around here—have you ever heard

of a manor with a name that ends in 'nell?'"

"Nope." He paused. "The guy who took this picture knew what he was doing. The lighting from the moon behind the clouds is really eye-catching."

Austin raised an eyebrow. The picture had been taken in full daylight. He decided not to say anything to his obviously less-intelligent roommate.

Nate walked over from the counter, carrying the cheese, bags of chips, and photograph. "What's up with the guy in the corner?"

Austin pulled one of the DVDs out of the sleeve and put it in the player. "There's no guy. It's probably a bush."

"Dude, I'm not blind—check it out."

After making sure the disk was set, Austin took the picture, glancing at it. Then he pulled it closer, frowning. Weird. How did he miss that? "The person wasn't there earlier—I swear. And it could be a guy or a girl. Too blurry to tell."

He looked up at the TV, watching the opening credits. He'd seen the picture just a couple of hours earlier and knew he wouldn't have missed something that noticeable. And Nate was right about another thing—the photograph was obviously taken at night. Had Austin been *that* distracted by the price?

80 • 08

The following evening, Nate hosted a party in their apartment, and he bribed Austin to come out of his room for most of it by telling him how much everyone wanted his white chicken chili. Apparently, several of Nate's friends had requested the stuff, and Nate didn't tell Austin this important detail until half an hour before the party.

Austin procrastinated and stressed over what to wear that would help him blend in more than usual, finally emerging long after the doorbell had rung the first time. If he'd had a say, he would've cooked the chili several hours earlier, then left it in the Crock-Pot so everyone could serve themselves, leaving him free to read in his room.

As expected, tons of people showed up. Nate was popular. But at least he'd invited Lizzie and her roommate, Nicole. Austin couldn't help but wonder if Nate had also invited Savannah. That would make things awkward.

Austin's hands start sweating as soon as Nicole arrived. She came into the kitchen section of the great room and smiled him.

Act normal. Act normal. "Hey, how's it going?" That was an okay question, right? He resisted the urge to wipe off his hands.

"Great! I hear you're cooking white chicken chili. Yours is the best, you know."

"Yeah." Lame. He didn't know what else to say.

He needed to come up with something to talk about before she moved on. School? No that would be dumb. He didn't want their relationship to revolve around classes. What about the weather? That was a safe topic, right? He opened his mouth, then clamped it shut right away. A relationship that revolved around clichéd conversation topics wasn't high on his list either.

Nicole didn't seem to sense his internal dilemma. "How was your Arete 101 exam? You took it yesterday, right?"

School it was, then. "Yes. It went well. I passed."

"Congratulations."

An expression he couldn't read crossed Nicole's face. Did she want to leave? Talk to him more? Was her boredom showing through or had he said something wrong?

To stop her from going somewhere else, Austin grabbed the picture from the counter where it had sat, ignored, since the night before. "You like art, right?"

"Mostly music, but yeah."

"Check this out. My brother sent it to me. It's pretty bad."

Nicole took the picture and cringed when she saw it. "Whoa. That's intense. And I wouldn't say it's bad—it's quite good, actually. And very, *very* creepy."

"Creepy?" That wasn't a word Austin would have used to describe it.

"Well, yeah. That guy—or woman—crawling across the grass like that. How did the photographer manage to capture this? It looks like it was taken in the late 1800s, and not many pictures from back then showed this sort of emotion. The artist was very skilled."

Before Austin could take the picture back to inspect it, Nicole turned away and showed it to Lizzie, whose reaction was similar, though stronger. Everything Lizzie did was a tad over the top.

Realizing he wouldn't see it again for a while,

Austin forgot the picture and focused on cutting chicken for the chili. But he kept tabs on Nicole as she wandered around the room, laughing with many of the other people. Whenever she talked with a guy, he paid extra attention. After a while, he breathed a sigh of relief. She didn't seem to like any of them, though several watched her closely and pounced as often as they could.

Then he noticed something that made him really happy—she sent glances his way every now and then. She had to be interested in him, right? They'd shared a kiss a while ago . . . but he knew well enough that kissing didn't always equal a relationship. His thoughts flicked to Savannah, his ex-girlfriend. She wanted to get back together again, and a part of him welcomed that idea. On the other hand . . . Nicole was nice and cute, and dating Savannah never went very well.

Austin grunted at himself and pushed aside all thoughts of girls, focusing on the chili. He quickly added the remainder of the ingredients to the Crock-Pot to heat before serving.

Someone bounced up beside him and he didn't need to look to know who it was. "Hey, Lizzie."

"Hey. When are you going to ask Nicole out?"

He froze. "Huh? What are you—"

"You watch her all the time. Your face lights up when she comes in the room." Lizzie leaned forward, putting her hands on the counter. She opened her mouth to say something else, but just then, Nate walked up, and grateful, Austin turned to talk to him.

"We have any more chips?" Nate asked. "And how

much longer until the chili is done?"

"An hour, probably. And here—take them." Austin pulled another bag from the cupboard and handed it to Nate who, unfortunately, left.

"I'm serious, Austin," Lizzie said when they were more or less alone. "You'd make a great couple. *Ask her out*." She pounded the counter top for effect.

Austin looked around quickly, hoping no one had heard, then turned back, trying to find a response. She didn't wait for him, though. Flashing an impish smile, she flipped her red curls and bounced back to the group.

A big breath rushed out of his lungs—he wasn't even aware he'd been holding it. His eyes automatically found Nicole's face in the crowd. She watched Lizzie, then looked across the room and met his gaze. His stomach clenched and he ducked, pretending to get something out of the cupboard below the counter.

$$\mathcal{SO} \bullet \mathcal{CR}$$

Later, after everyone left, Austin finally remembered the picture and what Nicole had said. He found it under a pile of blankets on one of the couches and sat down, holding it to the light. Then he nearly dropped it.

Not possible. Not possible at all.

Wanting to do the opposite, he brought the frame closer, staring at its contents.

Nicole was right.

About ten feet from the camera and crouched down on all fours was a person, looking at the manor. It was grotesque and skeletal. Bones jutted out, almost appearing to be broken. The body was wrapped in scant amounts of worn black cloth—cloth that looked worm-eaten. Stringy, dirty hair fell from a nearly bald scalp. The skin was pale, translucent.

A strange feeling hit Austin—the creature meant to do harm to the people living in the manor. He wasn't sure how, but he knew that. He cringed, trying not to think about it.

Where did the figure come from? And where was the head that had been in the bottom right corner?

He lowered the picture and stared at the wall in front of him. Maybe he'd imagined things. Maybe everyone else had, too.

Austin counted to thirty before glancing down.

The person was still there.

What if the creature could get out of the frame?

Austin jumped up, holding the corner of the picture, and strode across the apartment to the empty bedroom where he put the photograph facedown in the bottom dresser drawer. He knew it was irrational, but he didn't want it anywhere near him.

With some effort, Austin pulled the heavy, solid oak bed frame in front of the dresser, then shut the doors to the room.

After a cursory glance around the apartment, he strode into his own bedroom and shut the door behind him, locking it.

℘ • ℭ

First thing the next morning, Austin sent a text

to Lizzie and asked her to come over as soon as she could. It was time to get some information about the photograph.

Lizzie called him right away without responding to the message. "What's up?"

"You saw that picture of the manor last night—I need to find out where the house is."

"Okay. I'll bring Nicole. We'll be there in a minute."

Nicole was coming! And they didn't live far away. Austin smoothed his shirt and combed his fingers through his hair, then grabbed a rag and wiped up the chili that had spilled onto the counter the night before. A few minutes later, the doorbell rang, and he invited Nicole and Lizzie inside. Nate emerged from his room, still in his pajamas.

"What's going on?" he asked.

Austin motioned to Nicole. "Tell him what you saw in the photograph."

Nicole sent Austin a curious expression, but did so, describing the figure and manor in detail. Austin watched Nate's reaction carefully and wasn't disappointed.

Nate abruptly sat on a stool, his jaw dangling. He didn't respond for a moment. "We're talking about the same thing, right? You're sure that's what you saw?"

"Of course." Nicole flipped her ponytail, obviously annoyed that he would question her.

Austin half smiled, then set aside his amusement and leaned against the counter. He explained to the girls what the picture looked like when he first got it, and then the change Nate had seen later. "We need to find the house," he said. "Something bad is going to happen to the people who live there. I can feel it."

Nate stood. He looked back and forth between Austin, Lizzie, and Nicole before letting his gaze settle on Lizzie. "Okay, don't hate me, but I really can't get involved in this. I'm struggling enough in school as it is, and all my spare time needs to go to studying."

Lizzie gave him a hug. "It's fine—go, do homework." She turned to Austin after Nate left and asked, "What information do you have on the house?"

"Just this." Austin pulled out a notebook where he'd described the manor and the changes in the picture. He'd put the description from the back of the photograph there as well.

"Nell Manor, Seattle . . ." Nicole chewed thoughtfully on her thumbnail. "Did you Google it?"

"Let's do that now."

Austin got his laptop and set it on the counter. The girls crowded around, watching as he typed in the words "Nell Manor, Seattle."

Nothing came up.

"That's weird," Lizzie said. "Google's never failed me before."

Nicole smiled, then tucked a strand of blond hair into her ponytail. "What's going on with the picture now? Any other changes?"

Austin shrugged. "Haven't looked at it since last night."

"Let's get it!" Lizzie said.

Austin hesitated for a moment, then led the way to

the guest bedroom.

Before opening the doors, though, he faced them. "Don't laugh—seeing that figure was really disturbing, so I locked it up."

He pushed the door open, half expecting someone to jump out at them. Of course no one did, and he strode across the room and shoved the bed aside, then pulled open the drawer where the frame still lay facedown. He picked it up and tucked it under his arm, walking back to the kitchen, then put it on the counter.

The three of them leaned forward to look at it.

Nicole gasped. "It *is* heading for the manor!"

And she was right. The figure had crept forward and was only a short distance from the house.

"But why?" Nicole looked up at Austin, her crystal-blue eyes filled with concern, the strand of hair falling out of her ponytail again.

Austin resisted the urge to reach out and brush the hair away, turning instead to the photograph. "Don't know." A million thoughts raced through his brain. Who was it? What were they planning to do? And why? Could they actually stop it if something bad really was about to happen there? "See, this is why I need to find out more about the place."

"I'll bet we can ask around at the university," Lizzie said. "Or check the library. There's got to be a listing of manors in Seattle—this place is as old as the city, after all."

The other two agreed, and they left. Austin brought the picture, keeping it in his backpack—hopefully it wouldn't change again anytime soon.

A storm was blowing in, the sky darker than usual. The wind picked up and leaves scattered across the sidewalks as the three friends quickly walked to the library.

Once they arrived, Nicole enlisted the help of a student librarian, and after a few moments, they found a huge book that cataloged old homes in Seattle.

Lizzie plopped down on a chair. "It's going to take forever to go through this."

"Probably," the librarian said. "Do you have any information on the house that would make it easier?"

Austin raised his eyebrow. Shouldn't that have been the first thing the librarian asked? He shrugged the question off, though. She probably hadn't been around long.

Nicole gave the girl a slip of paper on which she'd written the words from the back of the photograph.

"Oh! Wonderful. We have an internal database that might be able to pull up this info." She turned to a computer, and after a few clicks, showed them the page numbers where houses with names ending in "nell" were listed in the book.

Nicole and Lizzie quickly divided the numbers between the two of them—Lizzie looking at those in the back, Nicole starting from the front. Austin smiled at them, leaning forward in his chair. He enjoyed researching, but wasn't about to get in Nicole's way.

A couple of moments later, Nicole said, "Ah-hah!" and whirled, yanking the volume from Lizzie's hands. She thanked the librarian, who walked back to her desk. "Let's compare the pictures."

Austin took out the photograph—nothing had

changed—and they put it next to the book. "That's the one," he said. The article labeled the place as "Britnell Manor." Austin jotted down the address, then turned to the girls. "Let's go check it out."

"Just a minute," Nicole said. She pulled out her phone and took a picture of the house in the book, along with the description beside it. "In case we need that later."

They hurried through the chilly wind to the parking area behind Austin's building and piled into his car. Nicole gave driving directions using the map on her phone, and after about twenty minutes of navigating Seattle's streets, they approached Britnell Manor's coordinates, according to the book.

"Trees, trees, trees," Lizzie said. "Don't people ever get tired of them? They make it impossible to see anything!"

The other two didn't respond. Austin craned his neck, looking down each driveway until he found a place on the left that looked exactly like the picture. The mailbox addresses on either side of the house confirmed it was the one. "There it is," he said, pointing. He turned the car around and pulled up in front, grabbed his backpack and met the girls on the gravel driveway.

No one said anything for a moment. The brisk wind whipped around them, making goose bumps rise on Austin's arms. He wasn't sure what he'd been expecting once they got there—to actually see the figure in the photograph?

"Where was the picture taken?" Nicole asked.

"Over there, I'd guess." Austin didn't move. It felt

like they were intruding. A slight magical vibration washed over him and he concentrated on it for a moment. He couldn't pinpoint the source, but it felt negative—bad. Evil, maybe.

Nicole zipped up her jacket. "This place gives me the creeps." She stared at the manor. "It's obviously empty. I wonder for how long."

Lizzie gasped, and Austin turned. She was pointing at a mound of dirt not far from the car, partially hidden from the street by shrubbery that lined the sidewalk. A hole was next to the pile.

Pushing the negative feeling aside, Austin hurried to the hole and looked in. He recoiled instantly and bumped into Nicole.

Black, decaying cloth peeked through the dirt along the edges of the deep pit. The scrapings in the sides of the hole showed it had been dug by fingers and not by a shovel. The dirt was still fresh.

Ignoring Nicole's warnings, Austin crouched down, holding his hand over the earth. He wanted to close his eyes to concentrate better, but didn't want to make himself that vulnerable.

Using his Earth Arete abilities, he focused on the soil. "Something violent happened here a long time ago." He squinted, focusing on another shred of information. "Mixed emotions—sadness, regret, envy. Much more recently, anger."

He stood, noticing that the grass on the side of the hole nearest the manor was smashed down, creating a trail which led toward the house. The negative sensation from a moment earlier returned, and even though it felt like a warning, he followed the trail until it stopped—fifteen feet from the house.

The magical waves hit him strongly, almost causing him to fall over.

"I . . ." He hesitated, trying to ignore the desire to run back to the car. "I think this is where the creature stopped last time we looked at the photograph."

He turned to the girls, the hair on his arms and back rising, and decided to voice his fears. "Can you feel that? It's . . . it's still here"

Nicole nodded, her face pale. She clutched his arm. "Do you have the photograph?"

"In my backpack." He pulled the bag down and removed the picture. The girls leaned over.

"The figure is gone," Nicole said. "Where did it go?"

"Oh, crap." Austin pointed at the manor in the photo. "The window is open—it wasn't before. The thing is inside."

They looked up at the actual house and Lizzie screamed. The trampled grass no longer ended where they stood, but now led all the way to the porch. And like in the picture, one of the windows was open.

Austin handed the photograph to Nicole. "We need to make sure no one's home!" He dashed forward.

"Austin, wait!" Nicole called. "It's dangerous!"

He didn't stop, not caring whether they followed or not. What if there were people inside? He had to do something!

He knocked frantically on the door. No one answered, so he tried the knob—locked.

"It's probably empty," Lizzie said as she and Nicole caught up.

Austin ran across the huge porch to the open window.

"What are you doing?" Nicole asked.

"Going in." Austin looked back at them. "We have to warn the owners."

"No, we don't!" Nicole said at the same time Lizzie cried for him to stop.

Austin again ignored them and pushed the window open the rest of the way. He swung his legs over the ledge and ducked under the frame.

The room was dim, and he had to wait for his eyes to adjust. Streams of muted light barely shone through windows that hadn't been washed in years. A few items throughout the room were covered with sheets. Cobwebs draped everywhere. A dead rat lay along the wall to his left. The wood floor was coated with at least an inch of dust. Then he noticed markings in the dust on the floor where something big had recently shuffled from the window. The tracks stopped four feet from him.

Magical pulses, so strong he felt like he should be able to hear them, washed over him. He put his hand on his pounding heart, remembering the last time he'd felt pulsations that strongly. It had been while in Arches National Park in Utah.

Austin took a breath of stale, musty air and moved to the side, letting the girls peer in through the window. He pointed to the floor. "The creature is right there."

"I can sense it," Nicole said.

"And he knows we're here, too." A strong wave hit him, and he backed against the wall. "Did you feel that? It just pushed against my magic. I . . . I think it wants us to leave."

Nicole and Lizzie stepped away from the window.

"That's a great idea," Lizzie said. She cleared her throat and reached in, grabbing Austin's arm, tugging him. "Besides, I have to take the Arete history test."

Austin nodded, but hesitated still. Lizzie's persistent yanking convinced him, though, and he climbed out the window, leaving it open behind him. The desires of that thing were completely clear—it wanted to be left alone while it completed its task.

Once they were in the car, Austin said, "I'm positive it's going to do harm to the place. We have to stop it."

Nicole shook her head. "I don't think we can—it happened in the past, back when the picture was taken."

He scowled. She might be right, but that wouldn't keep him from returning. He at least had to try.

₭ ♦ ℞

Austin pulled the picture out of the backpack and laid it on the kitchen counter without looking at it. He didn't want to know if there were any changes. He and Nate had a study session, and Nate was already impatient.

"Thanks for coming with me," Nate said. "The Arete exam isn't going to be pretty, and this session today should really help. I've heard the TA who'll be conducting it is really good."

Austin didn't reply. He couldn't keep his mind off

Britnell manor and the figure they'd followed inside. What had happened there so long ago? And were they sure it was in the past? What if the picture showed the future? He dismissed that idea as quickly as it came to him.

The TA took things too slowly, and Austin, bored the entire time, doodled in his notebook. But Nate got a lot out of it and talked constantly on the way home. Austin had a hard time following the one-way conversation until Nate asked a direct question.

"Did you see what he did with that clod of dirt?"

Austin rolled his eyes. "Yes, and I could do that before even entering the university."

"I'm not surprised," Nate mumbled.

Most Aretes didn't come to their power until around eighteen years of age, which was why they didn't enter Arete universities until that time. But Austin had always been somewhat ahead of the others. His Restart—the moment when an Arete's powers manifest themselves—had happened at fifteen. It was nearly unheard of, and his parents had hired a private Earth Arete tutor. Austin learned quickly from the woman. By the time he turned sixteen, he could already move several pounds of dirt at a time, and at eighteen, he could control vast quantities of dirt, along with aspects of the other elements. Most Earth Aretes at eighteen still struggled with a teaspoonful of dirt.

"Why aren't you a tutor? Why aren't *you* up in front of everyone?"

Austin's hands instantly started shaking. He tucked them into his jacket pockets, hoping Nate hadn't noticed. Him? Stand in front of a large group of people? He'd rather jump off a bridge. He shook his head. "It's his job, not mine."

Nate didn't say anything else, and they got back to their apartment building a few minutes later.

"Why's our door unlocked?" Nate asked.

Austin's thoughts instantly jumped to the safety of the photograph, and he rushed down the hall to the kitchen area. He stopped abruptly.

"Mark? What are you doing?"

The RA for the building yelled in shock and turned from the stool where he'd been sitting. "Nothing. Just . . ." His eyes flicked around the room, barely resting on Nate and Austin, then shifted away. "Just doing apartment checks. Everything looks good." He glanced down at the picture clenched in his hands.

"Give that to me." Austin motioned to it.

Mark stared at it a moment longer, then put it on the counter. "You shouldn't have something like that around. Freaked me out. There's a bad feeling in it. Does Professor Coolidge know you have it?"

Austin pointed down the hall toward the front door. "Time for you to go—we have homework to do."

He waited until the RA left, then looked at the picture and felt the blood leave his face.

"Holy . . ."

Nate joined him. "Oh, wow."

The figure was at the window, staring straight into the camera—at the viewer. The expression was distorted into a glare, hair tumbling down one side of the face, skeletal fingers gripping the curtains on either side. Austin's hands shook so hard he was glad he wasn't holding the picture. "It's looking at us—it sees us!" He turned to Nate, grateful not to be alone. "I think it's a warning for me not to go back."

Nate's eyebrows shot up. "You actually *went* there? Why would you do that?" He backed away. "This is getting really weird," he said, then strode to his room.

Austin pulled his cell phone out of his pocket and dialed Cody's number.

"What on earth did you send me?"

Cody chuckled. "Imagine how I felt! I watched it go through an entire cycle twice. Where in the . . . uh, *vision* . . . are you?"

"The creature thing is looking out the window and staring straight at the camera."

"What? It is? It never did that before. What did you do?"

Austin shook his head. "We might have messed it all up. We found the place and went inside. Cody, the thing knew I was there! It pushed against my magic. It wanted me to leave."

"Whoa, man. How come you did that? I wanted you to find info on the manor, but I didn't expect you to actually go there!"

"Why wouldn't I? Isn't that part of gathering information?"

"Um, no, dude. And I bet the photograph won't follow the cycle I saw again." He abruptly changed the subject, talking about girls and school for a moment. After a couple minutes, he said he had to go. "Oh, and . . . Austin?"

"Yeah?"

"Do me a favor and don't be stupid."

"All right, I won't."

After they hung up, Austin called Lizzie. She didn't answer. "Call me back as soon as you can. Actually, just grab Nicole and come over. Something's changed with the picture. And it's not good."

Lizzie and Nicole arrived an hour later, and Austin showed them the photograph.

Nicole held it, head tilted. "Nothing's really going on." She paused. "Other than the window not being open anymore."

Austin snatched it from her. The window was closed, and so were the curtains. "The drapes are shut. They weren't before." He quickly told them about the figure looking at the camera. Then he brought up his conversation with Cody. "If going there changed things, it might mean we can prevent the creature from doing something bad!"

Lizzie frowned. "But how do we know something bad *will* happen?"

"I felt it—I felt the malice." Austin started to pace, thinking. They needed to protect the house, and especially the people who had lived there. The place had been well cared for during the time the photograph was taken—obviously, the owner would want it to stay safe. But what could Austin and the girls do on their own? The magic behind that creature was strong—stronger than Austin's magic.

They would need help. They'd have to gather a group of Aretes who could work together. That way, they'd keep the creature from causing harm to the manor.

He turned to the girls and told them his thoughts, then asked Nicole, "Do you still have the picture you took of the manor's entry in the book?"

"Yeah, here on my phone." She pulled it out and loaded the photo. "Got it."

"Read the description out loud."

She squinted, holding the phone close, probably trying to read the tiny print. "It says that the owner, Mr. Britnell, died alone a couple years after his wife and infant son disappeared. People thought they were kidnapped or something, and it broke his heart. Then there's other stuff about how big the place is, and what Mr. Britnell did for a living. He owned a fishing company."

Austin didn't respond. He stared out the window, watching students walk past. "I'll bet the figure from the photograph is about to kidnap Britnell's wife and child."

Lizzie squealed, hands over her mouth, making the others jump. "We have to do something! We have to stop the guy before he gets to them!"

"Whoa, hold on," Nicole said. "Are we sure we want to get involved?"

Austin shook his head. "I'm with Lizzie—we have to at least try. And we're going to need every Arete student we know—we'll tell them it's practice."

"How are we going to use our abilities to stop him?" Lizzie asked. "I don't think me starting the place on fire will do any good."

Austin paced again. "We'll focus on our magic itself—the foundations of our individual powers. Since the figure is in the house now, we'll keep pressure on him, holding him there until we can convince him to leave the wife and boy alone."

80 ◆ CR

Gathering Aretes took a lot longer than Austin expected, and by the time everyone met up at his place and left for the manor, the sun was an hour from setting. The group was small—only seven students. Most of the other students Nicole and Lizzie had contacted, including Savannah, were taking midterms or studying and couldn't come until later. Coolidge, the only professor any of them had been comfortable asking was on a date with his wife.

Nicole insisted on driving this time, and Austin sat in the front seat. They were followed by a few other cars of students.

Feeling the need to do so, knowing there would be a change, Austin grabbed the photograph. "Uh . . . guys? The picture's changed again."

"What's different?" Lizzie asked from the back.

"He closed another set of curtains. Look." Austin handed the picture to her.

Nicole's hands turned white on the steering wheel. "I just realized something."

Austin looked at her, momentarily distracted by the way the sunlight danced across her face. She was so pretty. He gave himself a mental shake, focusing again on the conversation. "What's that?"

"The changes are happening faster. The intervals— they're speeding up."

Austin faced ahead, his eyebrows knitting. She was right. Before, transformations would happen after several hours. But now? Between seeing the figure at the window and both sets of drapes closing, it had only been an hour.

"We've got to hurry," he said. "There might not be enough time to save the kid if we don't."

Nicole stepped on the gas and pulled around a couple of cars, ignoring their honks.

A few moments later, they arrived at the manor, piled out, and met the rest of the students on the driveway. Austin scanned the place. Both curtains were shut and the hole by the street was still there, grass still trampled. He was glad the storm from earlier had blown through, leaving what should be a clear, moonlit night—an oddity in Seattle. But it would help to have the extra light.

Everyone turned to Austin, waiting expectantly. He cleared his throat, feeling his cheeks start to burn. "Nicole? Lizzie? Can we talk for a moment?" They stepped away from the others. "Would you two arrange everyone around the house? I want to check out a few things. Oh, and while you're at it, let them know we'll be using our power to push against the magic of the guy inside. It'll take some getting used to, but I think everyone here should be able to do it."

Lizzie raised her hand. "I'll organize the Aretes if Nicole will tell them what to do."

Austin looked to Nicole—she agreed. "And Nicole, make sure anyone else who comes knows the plan, if you wouldn't mind."

He jogged back to Nicole's unlocked car, where he'd left his backpack, and pulled out the photograph, wanting to keep it with him. Back at the manor, Lizzie assigned him to a window near Nicole. That made him smile—he knew what she was up to, and he was mostly okay with it. As long as Lizzie didn't put him on the spot again, like at the party the night before.

He checked the photograph every five minutes, though he wasn't entirely sure how doing so would help him.

A few more people showed up, which gave him some confidence. This wouldn't be difficult if they had enough support. Right?

Twenty minutes after they got to the manor, another set of curtains on the main floor shut, both in the picture and the real house. Ten minutes later, drapes on the second floor were closed.

Austin paced, keeping his powers pressing into the manor, wondering if they were making things worse by getting involved. He ignored that thought. Too late now, and he'd rather try to save the baby.

He started to notice a pattern. The creature—man-thing—was only shutting curtains here and there. It had to be because he wanted privacy. He wanted to be able to get upstairs and back down again without someone watching him from the outside. Austin shook his head, wondering what his brother had seen and why Cody wouldn't tell him. Apparently, it wasn't any of this.

An hour after sundown, the Aretes near Austin jumped in surprise. He barely noticed them—a strong sensation had just flooded over him, pushing against his powers. The warning was impossible to ignore: Leave. Now.

"It's almost time!" Austin said to Nicole. "Tell them to start sending the message to leave the family alone."

She passed the word to the Aretes around her, and he felt the pulsings around them rise as they increased their magical push, matching the strength of the creature inside.

He looked at the picture again, using his cell phone for light. By then, he was used to seeing disturbing things, but this time, what he saw actually made him drop the picture.

Once again the figure was staring out a window at the viewer. At Austin. But this time, he was holding a baby and grinning. The expression was obviously one of triumph. Of having succeeded.

And Austin realized something. The man didn't need to take the baby away to do harm—he could murder it right then and there.

"He's gonna kill the baby!" Austin yelled. "I'm going inside to stop him."

Nicole grabbed his arm. "No!"

He sidestepped her and flung the window open, ducked under the frame, then turned to face her. "Keep the Aretes going—don't let them lower their magic. We have him, I know we do."

She hesitated, then nodded. Austin turned around, holding his cell phone in front of him, using the flashlight application. He gave his eyes a moment to adjust to the dim light, but then, quietly as he could, followed the marks on the floor. They led him out of the room and across a grand entry to a marble staircase. He didn't have to see any more of the place to know it had been very beautiful in its prime.

Austin took the stairs two at a time and turned to the right, following the prints. He sprinted down a hall and to the base of another set of stairs. The traces in the dust led him up to the third floor, and again he followed. They stopped in front of a closed door to at the right.

Holding his breath, he pressed his ear up against the wood, trying to make out any sounds.

Nothing.

He wished he'd brought the photograph—it might have given him a clue as to what was going on inside the room.

He felt a faint magical vibration originating from within—the man didn't seem to know Austin was there. Or had he left already, and Austin was confused?

No. The creature *had* to be there.

Deciding there wasn't anything else he could do, Austin pocketed his cell phone. He turned the knob and slowly pushed the door open.

It creaked, of course—he'd been expecting that, but he started just the same. He didn't enter, scanning the space before him. No one was there. The room was obviously a nursery, lit by the pale moonlight, little toys and stuffed animals everywhere. Had no one cleaned up after the baby was kidnapped?

Austin concentrated on the pulse in the room—he was positive the nursery wasn't empty. But would he be able to see anything?

Then he noticed something odd about the drapes—

the way they had been lifted up without a sash or tie. It was as if something he couldn't see kept them there.

He gasped, realizing the creature was holding them.

Suddenly they fell. A shape flicked into full view. A beautiful woman turned to face him, holding a sleeping infant in her arms. Her eyes were sad, lonely, and she seemed to stare right through him. But then she looked down at the child, a smile played across her lips, and her features warmed.

Austin held perfectly still. He was hallucinating—that was the only explanation. People didn't just appear out of thin air. Maybe the creature was in a different room? He took a step back, hand on the knob.

The woman looked up at him abruptly, seeming shocked to find him there. Her features contorted, a sneer stretching her lips, her skin changing texture and appearance until instead of the blond from just moments ago, the figure from the photograph was before him. Grotesque, skeletal hands encircled the baby.

It wasn't a man who'd kidnapped the infant—it was a woman.

Austin slammed the door shut, holding it closed as hard as he could. Panic nearly overwhelmed him—his heart beating erratically, his breath coming in gasps. Sweat stung his eyes, dripping down his face.

The magical push grew stronger and stronger. Was she approaching the door, or just getting angry?

The knob in his hands started to burn—not with heat, but with magical energy. She was trying to get out. Austin didn't let go.

Suddenly, the feeling went away. The pulses retreated—faded. He'd won! He'd actually done it. He breathed a sigh of relief, leaning his forehead against the cool wood.

But then, Austin felt someone behind him.

He turned.

A man stood in the hallway, barely visible, sobbing, holding a book in his hands. His skin was partially rotted—his hair falling out. But there was life in his eyes. "Please, help me. I didn't know what I was doing! I didn't mean—didn't mean it! She won't forgive—won't move on." He took a shuddering breath, and an expression of intense agony crossed his face. "She's stealing my baby!"

"I . . . I . . ." What was Austin to say to a man who'd been dead for over a hundred years and was now there, in Britnell Manor, conversing with him? Had Austin completely lost his mind?

The guy tried to give the book to Austin. "Take it! Please! It's my diary."

Austin hesitated, then accepted the leather-bound journal, putting it in his pocket.

Relief flooded the man's features. "Thank you. Oh, thank you." He pointed at the door. "Keep her inside! She's still there, waiting. Don't let her go."

Austin nodded and turned his attention back to the nursery. He put his hands on the knob, feeling as the vibrations inside started to increase, the anger behind them boiling up, washing over him. He focused his own powers, matching hers—sending a clear message to leave the baby alone.

The handle grew hot again, and the pulses became strong. Much, much stronger—more than he could hold on his own. He felt his defenses weakening. What would happen if she broke through his magic? Would it destroy him?

"How do I stop her?" he asked the man. There wasn't a response.

Austin looked down the hall—it was empty.

He was alone.

Realization dawned on him. There was *no* way he'd be able to keep her there by himself. The magic she held was much more powerful than his—she hadn't started trying yet. He had no idea what he was dealing with, or who she was, really. How *stupid* it was to come inside alone!

The throbbing at the door grew to such an intensity that he nearly blacked out. He needed help! He had to get to the others.

Austin tore his hands from the knob and staggered away, then ran down the steps to the second floor.

A blast from behind nearly caused him to fall. She was coming!

Seconds later, he reached the bottom of the next set of stairs. He ran across the marble entryway, into the room with the open window, then lurched out, falling to the porch floor. He whirled on his knees and slammed the window shut. Nicole and Lizzie were there, crying. They threw their arms around him, others watching with concern, but he shook his head.

"Help me hold her in! She's coming now! Push with your magic!"

Austin braced himself mentally, reaching outward

with every ounce of his powers, trying to keep the woman inside the house—trying to stop her from stealing the baby. He felt his power strengthen as the others joined him again.

The force within the manor seemed to grow in might. She tested the edge of the Aretes' magic, trying to find weak spots. Austin smiled grimly when she pulled back. "That's right, freak," he whispered.

Then she attacked so forcefully that Austin heard several people gasp. A light flashed inside the manor, spinning around and around, faster and faster, making him dizzy. He had to turn away. Without warning, an incredibly powerful wave of magic hit all the Aretes at once.

They weren't strong enough.

A massive blast lifted everyone several feet into the air. They didn't drop—something held them. Then the windows of the manor exploded outward, glass and wood flying everywhere. The woman, beautiful again, stepped forward, glaring. With a small flick of her hand, she shot the students away.

Austin felt himself hit the ground. Another magical pulse smacked into him, freezing every muscle in his body. He couldn't even move his eyes, staring up into the night sky.

He heard her approach. Saw as she walked past, glaring down at him, a smile on her lips. Her skin changed color and texture, returning to the appearance of the worm-eaten figure from the photograph.

Then the pressure on him released. He jumped to his feet.

The others were also getting up, but Austin ignored

them, trying to find the woman.

He saw her then, crawling across the grass, holding something in her right arm. Just as she reached the hole at the edge of the lawn, she turned. He knew she was staring at him again.

A slight magical vibration washed over him. A hint of arrogance, some pity. But relief. Mostly relief. He got the distinct feeling that she would now be able to rest in peace. As he watched, she lowered herself into the hole, cradling the baby to her chest.

Austin hadn't realized it, but Nicole and Lizzie were trying to talk to him. He turned away from the woman, giving them his attention.

"What happened?" Lizzie asked.

"I still can't believe you got out alive!" Nicole stared up at him.

Austin ran his hand through his hair. "She won."

"She did? Oh, no!" Lizzie wailed, but then she frowned. "I noticed it was a woman. Can't blame us for thinking it was a guy."

Austin nodded. "She just crawled back into the hole. Let's go check it out—make sure everything is over."

Nicole put her hand on his arm. "Lead the way."

The three friends walked slowly across the grass, following the trampled trail. The closer to the hole they got, the less discernible the path was until finally, it disappeared. And when they arrived where the hole was supposed to be, it wasn't there. No uneven dirt, no slight bump. Just overgrown vines and grass.

Austin held his hand over the spot where he was sure the pit had been. What he felt didn't surprise him so much. That faint trace of violence was still there, but nothing had been touched in many years.

"It's over. All of it." He took a deep breath, incredibly grateful they were alive. If the woman had wanted to, she could have killed them.

They headed back to the manor where the others were grouping. Austin wasn't surprised to see that house was back to how it had been the first time they'd come—drapes open, windows shut. No sign that things had exploded when the woman forced her way out.

Austin picked up the photograph. It was once again a picture of a boring, Victorian-styled manor. He scratched his head, wondering if every single thing had been undone. Then he remembered the journal, and thrust his hand into his pocket. It was there! He pulled it out, turning it in his hands.

"What's that?" Lizzie asked.

He glanced at her. "Mr. Britnell gave it to me while I was inside."

Nicole tapped the side of her cheek thoughtfully. "He's been dead for a hundred years, at least. You're sure it was him?"

Austin nodded. He was about to open the leather book, but decided against it. "Let's get everyone back to the university. The three of us will read this together when the rest have gone home."

Nicole turned to talk to the other Aretes, but then she asked Austin, "Should we invite them over for root beer floats or something as a way to say thank you?"

"That's an excellent idea. And if anyone has

questions, we'll answer them while we're at it."

Two hours later—well into the night—everyone finally left. They believed Austin's account of the photograph. Maybe seeing a manor practically explode, then return to normal within a few minutes, was evidence enough.

Austin and the girls waited until the students had all left before they sat at the counter, crowding around the journal. Austin read it out loud.

Tom has returned with a huge load of fish. I'm grateful to have him running the company while I care for Elizabeth. She'll have our third child soon. Hoping it is a boy. Either way, I'm grateful to have so many children!

Another girl. A third girl! I didn't realize until today how much I wanted a son. I must have an heir to inherit the fishing company and Britnell Manor. But Elizabeth is tired—she doesn't want a Fourth. Says their magic is too much to deal with right now. But she's a Fourth—not sure why the idea is so hard for her.

Tom has sailed away again. I miss my best friend, but I'm sure he'll make another lucrative trip for the company.

Elizabeth is expecting! We're to have an Arete after all! I'm ecstatic with the possibilities! If only it's a son with my red hair. Always wished I'd had the power of fire.

Lizzie laughed. "Power to the redheads!"

Nicole shushed her and indicated for Austin to continue reading.

A boy! It's a boy! Oh, how wondrous! My company and manor are secured! I almost don't even care what color hair he'll end up having.

Little John Jr. does indeed have red hair. And his father's nose. And chin. Poor child.

He's nearing six months, and smiles a lot. The apple of my eye is he! But I'm worried about Elizabeth. She's been distant lately. Is she ill? She refuses to see a doctor.

Austin stopped reading, scanning ahead. "Oh, that's not good."

"What?" Lizzie asked.

"Listen."

My heart has been ripped from my chest! My soul burns within me. So full of anger. And the pain! Elizabeth and Tom . . . I can't even pen what I know they've done.

"Oh, how awful!" Nicole said. "Poor Mr. Britnell!"

Austin nodded, then continued reading.

It's been over a year since I last looked upon this diary. Doc says I'm close to dying, and it seems right, after all that has happened. All that I've kept inside me, until now.

I killed Elizabeth.

It wasn't on purpose. I pushed her away when she asked—no, begged—for forgiveness. She fell down her beloved marble stairs and hit her head, then didn't wake up. It was evening—the servants all in bed. Without telling anyone, I buried her on the edge of the property. Tom ran the morning she died, after I confronted him. No one has heard from him. The people of Seattle suspect he kidnapped or killed Elizabeth. They won't ever know the truth.

And it still burns my soul with grief and pain to write it, but two days after Elizabeth's death, my beautiful son was taken from me while he slept in his nursery. My poor, poor son. How I miss him! How I miss Elizabeth. I wish I could hold her in my arms— give her the forgiveness she sought.

"Whoa," Lizzie said. "A ghost kidnapped the baby!"

"It wasn't a ghost." Austin shook his head. "What we saw definitely wasn't that—it was Elizabeth, in her real body."

"That's disgusting."

Austin and Nicole agreed with Lizzie, then Nicole frowned, looking at Austin. "But why did Mr. Britnell want you to have the journal?"

Austin didn't respond at first. He had no idea. "Maybe he hoped I'd be able to contact her, let her know that he didn't mean to kill her?"

Lizzie tucked a thick strand of red curls behind her ear. "Yes—that must have been it." She sighed in exasperation. "I'm just annoyed that after everything we did, she still got the baby. I tried so hard to stop her—we all did—and we still failed! I hate feeling powerless."

Austin rubbed his eyes—the exhaustion was really catching up with him. "Same, and it was humbling. I don't think we alone could have made a dent. When she blasted us away from the manor, I felt just a little of her abilities and the vastness behind them. She was toying with us."

"Either way," Lizzie said, "over a hundred years have passed. It's gotta be too late to try to make things right for Mr. Britnell."

Austin nodded. "It might be. I'll watch the picture. When it starts the cycle over again, I'll go back to the manor to talk to her."

"And we'll come," Nicole said, smiling at him.

He said goodbye to the girls, then took the picture and journal to his room and placed both on his desk where he'd be able to see them every day.

But the photograph never changed again.

THE ANGEL

DEDICATION

To Lon Pearson
For his support, help, and friendship

THE ANGEL

ဆာ ✦ ର

Lizzie stepped out of the car and looked up in shock at the statue that "welcomed" her to the Smith family summer cabin. It was beautiful, but disturbing. The expression on the woman's face, the position— everything about her showed possessiveness. She reached toward the cabin, palm up, as if to beckon, but her smile, although alluring, made it obvious she wouldn't take rejection lightly.

Steph, the cabin owner's wife, paused next to Lizzie. "Let's grab your bags and I'll show you where you'll be stay—" She stopped, seeming to notice that Lizzie wasn't paying attention. "Dorothy. You there?"

Lizzie started at the sound of her real name and turned to the woman. "Call me Lizzie, please." She hesitated. "This statue . . ."

Steph smiled. "Is interesting, isn't it?"

Lizzie nodded.

"She was named Helen and was a powerful Arete from a very long time ago. The story says that Helen fell in love with a non-magical man who wouldn't have her, no matter how much she begged. They say she's still waiting for him to call for her. My husband found the statue near Crescent Bay and put it here to guard the house—he calls it our angel." Steph sighed. "Wish he'd just get rid of the dang thing. It gives me the creeps."

"Yeah, no kidding."

"All right, enough gawking. Let's go."

Lizzie pulled her bag from the back of Steph's Lexus. When she'd moved to Seattle to attend Katon University, she'd learned that most Arete students came from wealthy families. At least, those who attended Katon, anyway. So she didn't blink an eye at the nice car, but a Lexus in her small Texas hometown would've caused quite a disturbance. For one thing, it wasn't a beat-up truck.

She hefted her bag to her shoulder and started to follow Steph, but stumbled, looking up at the "cabin" where she'd be staying for the next week. It looked more like a Waldorf Astoria ski lodge than anything— endless windows and corners and rooms and what looked like three or even four levels. Was it really a one-family summer cabin or had she heard wrong?

She couldn't have heard wrong. Her friend had been very clear that his parents—and his parents only—owned it. Either way, she looked forward to relaxing after the stressful exams she'd just passed.

Lizzie had to jog to catch up with Steph, who led her past the two-story front doors and through a massive entryway lined with marble pillars. There was a rustic feel to the place—even though it was made with elaborate and expensive materials. The dark wood circular staircases on either side of the entry and the wooden flooring were striking in comparison to the marble. Rust-red decorations adorned the area, and heavy picture frames hung on the walls.

Lizzie followed Steph up the stairs to the left and down a hall to another set of stairs. Lush carpet cushioned her steps, replacing the wood flooring of before. The third-floor hall was lined with windows, and Lizzie looked out them in awe at the forest of Olympic National Park as she walked.

Finally, they reached the place where she would be staying. She stopped between the French doors that opened into the massive bedroom which was complete with two queen-sized beds, a coffered ceiling, and chandeliers. Decorative candles and fabric graced the dressers. The floor was rustic wood, scuffed up to look old. Soft-colored plush rugs were scattered throughout. And like the hallway, one wall was lined with windows. The pines parted enough to give an impressive view of Lake Crescent.

"Wow," Lizzie mouthed. She took a step inside and squealed, turning back to Steph. "This is amazing!" She dashed to the bed nearest the window, dropped her stuff on it, then spun around. "Thank you so, so much for letting me stay here!"

Steph smiled at Lizzie's enthusiasm. "I'm sure you need the break. Katon University is more stressful than other Arete universities."

Lizzie nodded. Being a magical person, an *Arete*,

was harder than regular people could know. On top of everything else those who attended college had to learn, Aretes had to perfect their magic and learn the science behind it.

Steph leaned against the door frame. "We're going for a hike after we have a snack. Would you like to come?"

"Sure!"

"Great. Sarah, your maid, will show you to the kitchen. Make yourself at home." She pulled the doors shut behind her.

"I've got a maid?" Lizzie whispered to herself. "Whoa." Weren't servants from the 1800s? Then she pushed her thoughts away, deciding to explore.

The windows were to the left of the doors and a sitting area was to the right, with the beds in the middle. Another set of French doors led from the sitting area into the biggest bathroom Lizzie had ever seen. Everything was made of marble—the floors, counters, and even the jetted tub. Gold accents adorned the place, and more elaborate candles dotted the room. And of course, there was a chandelier.

Lizzie returned to the main room and plopped on her bed, staring out the window. She'd text her best friend, Nicole, later, but right then, the only thing she wanted was to soak in the elegance she'd be living in for a whole week.

ЅꙆ ◆ ᏄᏄ

Lizzie jumped when someone knocked. A slender girl, several inches taller than Lizzie's five-foot-three frame, smiled when Lizzie opened to her.

"My name is Sarah. I'll be taking care of you and keeping your room tidy this week. Would you like me to show you the way to the kitchen?"

"Yeah, thanks." Lizzie paused, looking down at what she wore—simple jeans and a bright pink top that clashed with her red hair. The drive from Seattle to Lake Crescent—including the ferry—had taken about three hours, so she hadn't worn her nicest clothes. At least she was wearing good shoes for hiking. "Am I dressed okay?"

Sarah laughed. "Of course—John and Steph are hardly picky when it comes to things like that."

Lizzie was surprised to hear that—their son, Nate, always said they were uptight. "Okay. Let's go!"

It took five minutes to walk to the kitchen. Lizzie was positive she'd never find her way back. Sarah chattered about several things—how everyone missed Nate, the fourth child in the family who was studying at Katon University; how she hadn't known until the last second that she'd be able to come to work at the summer cabin; about her little kid; and a whole bunch of other things—Lizzie couldn't keep up with them.

Once seated at a table in the kitchen and after the blessing on the food had been given, Steph put her hand on Lizzie's arm.

"We're going up to Pyramid Mountain Trail. It gives an excellent view of the lake, but it's a long hike. Are you fine with that? If not, we can do a different one."

Lizzie smiled. Her mother would not agree with such an activity for a dancer. "Oh, yeah, I love hiking."

And Lizzie hated dancing.

"Okay. Later this week we'll also be going fishing, canoeing, and boating, if possible. I'd like to hike more than once, but we'll see how today goes first."

A few minutes later, Lizzie and members of Steph's family who'd arrived earlier met out front, where Steph divided them into the cars that would take them to the trail head.

Even though she always stayed at the front when hiking with a group, Lizzie now found herself drifting to the back, enjoying the beautiful surroundings. Washington had so much more to offer than Texas when it came to the color green.

Lizzie paused while staring into the forest to the left. She thought she'd just seen a structure of some sort. She backed up on the trail until her eyes found it again. It looked like a cabin—a real one, not like the Smith's mansion. She took a couple of steps closer, standing on the edge of the trail.

The cabin was moss covered and incredibly old. The wood looked to have been almost destroyed by the frequent moisture of the area. And it was so covered with undergrowth, a person wouldn't see it if they weren't looking directly at it.

Lizzie bit her lip, glancing up the trail to where she could see the others disappearing around a bend. They wouldn't notice if she took a brief detour to explore, and she was a good hiker. She'd have no problem catching up.

She started toward the cabin, her heart somersaulting in her chest. If there'd been a path, it had disappeared years ago. What sunlight there was diminished as soon as she entered the forest. Eerie light cast shadows all around her, making her skin tingle. Or maybe it wasn't the shadows. Maybe it was a magical awareness—something drawing her to the cabin. She couldn't really tell. She wasn't as adept at sensing magical pulses as Austin and Nicole, her good friends.

Lizzie climbed over slippery logs and boulders, nearly falling several times. Like the cabin, everything on the ground was covered in moss.

Her mom would kill her if she knew what Lizzie was doing. "Dancers protect their bodies from harm. You shouldn't do anything that would jeopardize your career."

Lizzie snorted. What her mom meant was, "You shouldn't do anything that would jeopardize my dreams of having a daughter with a dancing career."

Whatever.

A small creek separated her from the cabin and she crossed it easily, coming to a stop just outside the door. If at all possible, the hairs on her neck stood up even more. There was something different about the place, something that called to her.

The cabin hadn't been touched in a long time. Lizzie circled it, trying to get a better understanding of it before entering.

Wait. Did she really plan to go in? She flipped her curls off her shoulder. No, of course not. She just wanted to see the place up close.

And she was about to leave when she felt a slight tug on her magic. She hesitated in surprise—it had been a while since something like that happened. Was there a magical thing or person inside, waiting to be discovered?

The desire to go in washed over her. She couldn't tell where it originated, but what harm could come of it? She pushed all caution behind her as she shoved the door open.

Lizzie hesitated in the frame, unable to distinguish anything. It was too dark to see even outlines. The moist air that greeted her smelled old, but not disgustingly so—it was like leather and licorice, which were some of her favorite scents.

The faint magical pulse drifted over her again.

"Hello?"

No answer. She sensed a presence, but couldn't tell from what source—alive or inanimate. Austin or Nicole would've been able to tell the difference and she scowled, wishing she were that good. Then she remembered something Austin taught her, and using her magic, she pushed out, trying to elicit a response.

Nothing happened.

According to Austin, this meant the magical source wasn't alive, or it was a person very good at hiding.

She took a deep breath, waiting just a moment longer. It couldn't be a person—no one was *that* patient. And either way, she'd be safe to use magic to make a fire so she could see. But how to create it?

She could use her dancing. That was, after all, the reason she'd studied ballet and ballroom and jazz for so long. Dancing was supposed to help her harness her powers.

But there wasn't a lot of room, and she hated dancing anyway. So she did what always worked when she didn't want to dance. She mimed holding a pencil in her right hand and held her left like it was paper, palm up. Using her forefinger and thumb, she pretended to draw a small fire on her skin, concentrating on creating a physical spark.

A tiny flame erupted on her palm and she lowered her hand, allowing her eyes to adjust. Naturally, the blaze didn't burn and only required a little power to keep it going.

She took a step inside, hand in front of her, peering around. The wood floor was soft and springy, and in places, rotted away. Animal traps lined the walls, and fur pellets were stacked everywhere.

"A trapper's cabin," Lizzie said to herself.

The room had two cots, a wood stove, a small table with two chairs, and a shelf along one wall that was covered in knickknacks. Lizzie approached it, exploring the items with her right hand while her left radiated light. An old comb with gunk on it—yuck. Some used candles. A couple of figurines. A candle holder. Old, moldy newspaper she avoided touching.

A slight breeze entered the cabin, lifting her curls off her shoulders. She turned, expecting to see the door moving. Instead, the wind swirled around her, and she watched as some damp papers were blown off the table, revealing a little box.

She crossed the room and lifted the container. It was locked, but the bolt was rusted and broke when she pried at the tiny padlock.

The magical pulse washed over her again, enticing,

begging her to finish opening the box when she hesitated. She lifted the lid, not sure what to expect. Disappointment flooded over her at what was inside.

Just an old-fashioned whistle—the size and shape of her index finger.

Lizzie shrugged. "Too bad. You could've been gold coins or something cool like that." Rather than returning the whistle to the box, though, she pocketed it and turned to leave the cabin.

Air whisked past her, moist, smelling like the ocean, and she thought she heard a sigh full of longing. Heartfelt. Forlorn.

Lizzie paused for a moment. It was like a presence had come and gone while she stood there. Like that presence was grateful she'd taken the whistle. She said, "You're welcome."

Releasing the magic of her fire, she let it fizzle out and left the cabin.

"Lizzie? Lizzie!"

"I'm here." Lizzie rushed back to the trail and nearly ran into Steph, who'd just started entering the forest.

"Oh, you found one of Sutherland's cabins."

"Sutherland?"

"He and a trapping partner discovered Lake Crescent a long time ago. Their cabins dot the forest surrounding it." Steph linked arms with Lizzie. "Glad to see you're okay. Let's catch up with the others— you're going to love the view."

Lizzie nodded, putting her energies back into the hike. Steph set a brisk pace, and pretty soon, Lizzie felt sweat dripping down her back.

Regardless of how sweaty and hot she was, she couldn't stop thinking about the whistle in her pocket. Her hand strayed there frequently, feeling the outline through her jeans. She'd take a better look at it later, when she had the chance.

They finally reached the top, and Steph was right—it was breathtaking. Lizzie had never seen a lake so beautiful, surrounded by such a vivid green forest. Even though the sky was still clouded over, the lighting was perfect and everyone took plenty of pictures, including Lizzie.

After a picnic and some lounging around, the group headed back.

⁗ • ⁗

Steph gave everyone half an hour to freshen up before dinner, and Lizzie had fun exploring the shower—the wall was lined with all kinds of knobs and levers. She hopped in and streams of water hit her from every angle, giving her body a much-needed massage. She dressed in dinner-appropriate clothes, or what she thought were appropriate: a black skirt and a blue top with ruffles.

At the table, Lizzie eagerly awaited dinner, swinging her feet. They barely reached the floor. Servers brought out bread and soup first, and everyone went quiet as they started eating.

Steph put her spoon down. "When does your friend come?"

Lizzie savored the delicious taste of zuppa toscana—one of her favorite soups—before responding. "Day after tomorrow. You'll just love Nicole—she's tall and pretty and mature."

"She'll be coming with my son Nate, right? And Nate's roommate—what's his name again?"

"Austin. He's a great guy and a really good friend."

Steph looked up in surprise when one of the other people at the table mumbled something. "Oh, I still haven't introduced you to everyone. I apologize—I should have done that this morning before we went hiking. Let's do that now."

She then pointed around the table, indicating people as she spoke about them. Nate had three older sisters and a younger brother. All of them were there, along with a couple of spouses and Steph's grandchildren. Lizzie stared at Nate's younger brother for a moment. She'd never met a fifth child before—it was rare for people to have three kids, let alone four. But a fifth? She couldn't help but wonder if the teenager had magic, too. Wasn't it just the fourth child, though? She'd have to ask Austin when he came—he was sure to know.

Then Steph turned her questioning back to Lizzie. "Were your parents happy to have a Fire Arete?"

"Not at first—my mom wanted me to be a Wind Arete, like my best friend, Nicole, who's a few months older than me. But I was born with red hair that just wouldn't ever turn blond, so she resigned herself to having a child with fire powers instead of wind."

Steph took a drink, then set the glass back down. "I can see why you're not attending the Arete university in Maine—that's far from home—but why did you choose Katon instead of the Texas university?"

"It's where Nicole wanted to go, and I wanted to be with her, so my parents and I scraped up the necessary cash."

"Mmm." Steph pushed her plate back, motioning for one of the servers to remove it. She stood and tucked a strand of hair behind her ear. "I'm ready for bed. I'll see you all in the morning."

ဆာ ◆ Ꮹ

Goodnights were exchanged and Lizzie went straight to her room. She wasn't ready for bed yet, though. Then she remembered the whistle, which sat on her dresser where she'd put it after the hike. It was pretty dirty, so she cleaned it in the sink, then held it up to the light. The thing still had magic—even now, she felt it. Who created it? And for what purpose?

Small symbols she hadn't noticed before were etched into the side. She looked closer, seeing that they were words.

Quis est iste qui venit

Lizzie frowned. It looked like Spanish, but different. Portuguese? No . . . Then it dawned on her. Latin. She ran to her bag and grabbed her laptop, connected to the Internet, then pulled up a search browser and typed in the Latin words, followed by "translate."

"Who is this that is coming," she read out loud.

She leaned back, folding her arms. Why on earth would that be on a whistle?

A smiled crept across her face as she thought of Sparky Ann, her childhood dog. Lizzie turned the whistle in her hands, wondering if it had been owned by Sutherland and if he'd used it to call his dog. She brought it to her lips and blew.

A pure, delicate note issued forth—prettier than anything a flute could possibly make. For a moment, she felt like she was about to black out. Instead, a scene or vision entered her mind. A tall blond woman, slender, with dark eyes, holding her hand toward a rugged-looking man who stood several feet away. They were on the shores of what appeared to be a huge lake or bay. The moon was bright.

The man seemed to hesitate at first, then he shook his head and turned away, and a disappointed, hurt expression crossed the woman's face.

The scene ended just then and Lizzie lowered her hand, wondering at the power of the little whistle. She just saw a vision. Weird. A melancholy feeling swept over her, and she found herself wishing she could comfort the woman. Why did the guy reject her?

Suddenly, a brisk wind howled at the window, interrupting her thoughts. She walked toward the glass, looking out. Storm clouds billowed overhead and lightning flashed once—twice—across the sky.

Remembering the whistle, she again brought it to her lips, hoping to see more of the woman and man.

The sound was louder this time, and not as melodic, but no picture followed.

As soon as the note ended, the wind crashed against her window so hard, she fell to the ground in shock. Lizzie looked outside, expecting to see broken trees littering the yard. For some reason, her gaze was drawn to the statue on the other side of the drive. She frowned. It looked like it was staring at her. But that wasn't possible—the statue had been situated with its gaze directed at the front door, three floors down.

Lizzie backed away from the window, not wanting to see anymore.

Just then, someone knocked, making her jump.

She fluffed her curls, straightened her shirt, then pulled the door open.

"Are you okay?" Steph asked. "We heard a banging and wondered if something happened."

"Oh, I'm fine." Lizzie felt a blush creep across her cheeks. "I did fall, though. Kinda embarrassing."

Steph smiled and walked into the room, heading for the bathroom. "Do you have enough towels? Blankets?"

"Yes, definitely. Thank you for checking."

The older woman turned back to Lizzie, a concerned expression on her face. "Well, all right. We're in the room next door if you do need anything, and Sarah will be coming by sometime in the morning to change your sheets. We'll have breakfast at nine."

Another gust of wind rushed past the windows, startling both Steph and Lizzie.

"Sounds like we've got a storm coming. Bundle up tight! The place gets a bit cold sometimes."

Lizzie shut the door behind Steph, then tucked herself into bed, doing her best not to look out the window.

Sleep did not come instantly. Lizzie spent several hours tossing and turning, trying to block out the angry wind. After forever, she gave up and stared at the coffered ceiling above, trying mental games to calm her brain down. But then her mind started playing tricks on her, and she thought she saw weird shapes crawling across the walls and ceiling.

She shut her eyes tight, pulling the blanket over her head. But still, sleep did not rescue her.

After another couple of hours, she threw the covers back in exasperation and turned on the bedside light.

A sudden splash of water on the window made her jump, and she yanked the pillow over her head. Was it the rain? Or had someone dumped a bucket of water on the glass? That seemed like an eccentric thing to do . . . Right? And how could they have done it that far off the ground?

When nothing more happened, Lizzie looked at the pane. The glass was dripping wet, but it wasn't raining. "Stop imagining things, Lizzie," she whispered.

Pushing away her fears, she walked toward the window. The trees swayed in the brisk breeze, but everything else was calm.

Without meaning to, she glanced at the statue and regretted it. She jumped away from the window, putting her back to the wall, breathing hard. "Whoa. Lizzie. Knock it off. Seriously. Calm down." But no matter what she told herself, she knew her eyes weren't deceiving her.

She peered around the corner just to be sure. The statue *was* looking at her and was *closer* to her window. How was that possible? And what's more, its robes looked like they were getting longer—actively getting longer. Almost as if they were alive and growing. The face with that alluring smile stared up at her, and it was almost as if the distance between Lizzie's room and the driveway had shortened, making her feel like she was on the second floor instead of the third, or like the ground was coming up to meet her.

She was going crazy.

Lizzie grabbed her cell phone and jumped back in bed, pulling the blanket over her head. She opened her Kindle application and loaded her favorite Jane Austen book, reading as fast as she could, trying to force creepy thoughts away with visions of Fredrick Wentworth.

ℰ ♦ ℭ

Sometime after that, and with no further disturbances, Lizzie finally fell asleep. The next morning, she dashed downstairs, eager for human company. But it seemed like no one had slept well—they were all grouchy.

Lizzie ate pancakes, bacon, and eggs, then returned to her room to shower and dress. Before hopping in the shower, she checked the statue. It was just like it had been the day before. She'd imagined everything, she was sure of it.

Someone knocked while she was doing her makeup, and she opened the door to find Sarah there.

"Did you want another blanket for the bed?"

"Sure—that would be great, actually. Come on in."

"Which bed do you want it on?"

Lizzie hesitated—weird that Sarah would ask that question—and pointed to the four-poster nearest the window. "The one I slept in."

"I made each this morning while you were at breakfast," Sarah said. "Wasn't sure why you used both of them, but that's fine—it's your room while you're here."

What? Both beds were messed up? How did Lizzie not notice something like that?

Sarah pulled back the comforter, unfolded the blanket, and spread it across the bed. She replaced the comforter, then turned back. Her cheeks flushed and she wouldn't meet Lizzie's eyes. "Ummm . . . I'm embarrassed to bring it up, but I put plastic under the sheets of the beds. I hope that doesn't bother or offend you, but the sheets of the other bed were soaking wet this morning and I didn't want either mattress to get ruined." Sarah looked down, then back at Lizzie. "My sister had bathroom problems at night until she was sixteen. If you struggle with that sort of thing—"

"No! I don't, I promise." Lizzie's mind raced, trying to figure things out while coming up with an appropriate explanation. "I might have been hot, though." Weak. So very weak. Especially since she'd asked for another blanket.

Sarah nodded in response, gave a quick smile, and left.

Lizzie stared at the four-posters for a moment. She knew she hadn't touched the other one. But it seemed weird for Sarah to lie about something that big. *Had* Lizzie slept there? She shook her head—she hadn't even been able to sleep more than a couple of hours in one spot, let alone two.

℘ · ℭ

The group went canoeing on the lake. Lizzie had never done it before, and she almost capsized the thing again and again. Each time, Steph, her canoeing partner, laughed. She didn't seem to mind Lizzie's clumsiness at all, and it surprised Lizzie how well they got along.

Steph adjusted her hat over her ponytail, then grabbed the oar again. "That was an intense storm that came through last night."

Lizzie didn't respond—she was having a hard time getting her paddle thing to go the right way. For a dancer, she sure was uncoordinated.

"There's an old legend around here that whenever it gets windy and rainy, someone whistled for it."

Lizzie paused and turned to face Steph, not caring that they would slow down and lose the lead they had on the rest of the group. "Whistled for it? What do you mean?"

"They say, if you whistle, you'll bring in a storm. The old fur trappers refused to do it for fear the weather would turn bad and the *angel* would come and take them away."

"The angel?"

"My husband's statue—Helen."

Lizzie felt a chill when she thought of the woman. "Doesn't she guard the cabin?"

"It's more of a possessive guarding. See, Helen fell in love with Sutherland, one of the original fur trappers around here—actually, I already told you his name. You found one of his cabins yesterday. Being a powerful Arete, she believed she deserved anything and everything she wanted, and she loved and wanted Sutherland. Legend says he didn't return that love. Heartbroken, she promised she would watch over him and the land until he changed his mind, and when he called for her, she would return and take him with her to her world—the place where everyone goes after they die."

Lizzie frowned, twisting the oar in her hands. "Meaning, she'd kill him."

Steph laughed. "Pretty much. I'm sure she wouldn't have thought of it that way, however. She was too far in love with him."

"So when someone whistles, it brings Helen in a storm?" Lizzie watched as the rest of the group caught up and passed them. She didn't care anymore—this was more important.

"That's what they say."

"And she'll come and take that person away."

Steph laughed again. "Yes, but come on—it's obviously not true." She spread her arms wide, closed her eyes, and lifted her face. "And such a beautiful place could never be haunted."

Lizzie looked around. It really was gorgeous, but she couldn't forget the legend. Had she called the Arete? "So, you know how I found that cabin?"

Steph nodded, indicating for Lizzie to start rowing again.

Lizzie jumped to comply, feeling somewhat embarrassed to have been slacking on the job. "While I was in there—"

"Oh, you did go inside, huh?"

"Yeah, I did. Hope that's okay." She bit her lip, waiting for a reprimand, but Steph didn't seem displeased and so she rushed on, wanting to tell someone what had happened. "Well, I found a whistle. Brought it back with me, and I blew on it. And it got really, really windy all of a sudden."

Steph softly chuckled. "And you think the whistle might have brought the storm."

Her tone was comforting, and it made Lizzie wish she and Nate could trade places—that she'd been born to this woman who was so very accepting, even of silly ideas.

Lizzie closed her eyes, not wanting to say anything.

Steph put her hand on Lizzie's shoulder. "I wouldn't worry about it. We've always had the occasional rough storm. It wasn't because of you."

Lizzie blew out a breath of pent-up air, feeling her muscles relax as she accepted Steph's response. How childish to have thought she'd had something to do with the storm, anyway.

"Just enjoy your time here—the weather is

wonderful! Take advantage of it."

"Oh, I will."

"Let's see if we can catch up with the rest, shall we?"

Steph started paddling ferociously and Lizzie leaned forward, matching her energy.

They didn't catch up with the others until they'd reached the shore By the time they got to the designated picnic spot, Lizzie's arms were about to fall off. She had no idea how she'd be able to row back to the other side of the lake when the time came.

Lunch had been cooked in Dutch ovens that someone had set up early that morning. The food was super delicious—potatoes, gravy, meat, carrots . . . heavenly. After eating, the group lounged around for a couple hours, chatting.

Lizzie was especially happy when she found out that John, Steph's husband, had arranged transportation for everyone back around the lake—they wouldn't have to cross the water again.

Steph laughed at the expression of glee on Lizzie's face. "Yeah, we're spoiled and a tad lazy—one way is enough for us."

By the time they got back around the lake and to the cabin, it was dinner time.

Lizzie trudged up the sidewalk to the cabin, absent-mindedly following Steph. She was nearly bowled over by a small child being chased by Sarah who stopped when she saw Lizzie.

"Oh, Lizzie." Sarah stared at her with a confused expression. "I thought you were in your room—least, someone is up there, looking out the window."

Steph frowned, looking at Lizzie. "Your friend isn't coming until tomorrow, right?"

Lizzie nodded, then felt a grin spread across her cheeks. Maybe Nicole had come early! She glanced around, but didn't see her friend's car. Not waiting for anyone else, she dashed into the cabin and up the two flights of stairs, down the hall and to her room. She pushed the door open.

"Nicole? Are you here?"

A blast of wet wind rushed past her, misting her all over.

The room was empty. Lizzie rushed into the bathroom—it too, was empty, and she returned to the main area, pausing in the middle. At that moment, she noticed that Nicole's bed was again messed up, and she approached it, eyebrow raised.

The sheets were wet. She bent to sniff them, but the liquid didn't smell like urine or sweat. A pungent odor wafted over her and she knitted her eyebrows, trying to place it. Sea water?

Steph walked into the room and paused near Lizzie. "No Nicole?"

"Nope. But look—the bed I *don't* sleep in is messed up and wet." She turned to Steph. "How well do you know Sarah?"

"She's my best friend's daughter. Her husband left a year ago, and she has a little kid. She's an excellent young woman. Why?"

Lizzie shook her head—she'd already dismissed Sarah as a potential culprit. But how was the bed getting wet? "Never mind." She walked across the large room to the window and jumped when her foot splashed in water. The entire floor by the pane was covered in at least an inch of liquid. "Steph! Everything's wet!"

Steph joined her and gasped. "What in the world. . . ?" Her mouth set in a firm line and she folded her arms. "I'll call Sarah. Let's get this cleaned up." She pulled out a cell phone, sent a text, then motioned for Lizzie to follow her into the bathroom, where she filled the younger woman's arms with towels.

They mopped up water from the floor, walls, and windows. Steph was worried about the dresser—it had been splashed, and some of the paint appeared to be swelling, warping. "It's my grandmother's— an antique. I'll be heartbroken if the damage is permanent."

Sarah joined and helped finish wiping things up, then she and Steph remade the bed while Lizzie searched the room to see if anything had been stolen.

"I don't understand," Sarah said. "Who was in here?" She finished straightening the comforter, then turned to face Lizzie. "I did see someone, but I thought it was you."

Lizzie twisted the ring she always wore on her right hand. Helen's face entered her mind, and she glanced out the window to the statue. It was normal.

Steph excused Sarah, then linked arms with Lizzie, walking her to the dining room. "We'll get this figured out. Do you want to change rooms in the meantime?"

Lizzie hesitated. If she really *had* called Helen, the woman could find her anywhere in the cabin. And what if this was just a practical joke? She scowled.

She'd never allowed herself to be pushed around, and she'd *never* lost in the prank arena. "I'll stay in the room."

Steph nodded. After dinner and a set of movies, she walked Lizzie back to the third floor. "You know where to find me if you need anything."

Lizzie hugged the woman. "Thanks. I appreciate it." She was about to shut the door when a thought crossed her mind. "Oh, I wanted to show you the whistle." She grabbed it from the dresser and handed it to Steph.

Steph looked at it. "What does it say?"

"It's Latin. 'Who is this that is coming?'"

"Odd." Steph handed it back, then put both hands on Lizzie's shoulders. "Listen to me. There's no reason to believe any of this happened because you blew on that thing. My feeling is that someone—one of my kids, perhaps—has chosen you as the object of some stupid joke." She sighed, releasing Lizzie. "We'll find out who it is soon enough." Then she said goodnight.

Lizzie made sure the door was closed, then turned to face the room. She felt like it had been violated, though she knew that was irrational. "Calm down, Lizzie. Nothing's going to happen. Nothing *is* happening." She glared at the window. If this was a prank, that person *really* had it coming when she finally caught them.

She settled in bed, reading more Jane Austen, letting herself be taken away to a time long ago. Around two in the morning, the text on her Kindle application started blurring as her eyes struggled to stay open. She turned off her lamp, eager to catch up on lost sleep from the night before.

After half an hour, though, she thrust her covers away and turned on the light. The moon was bright and had been shining on her, preventing her from relaxing. Some vacation this was turning out to be. And why weren't there curtains, anyway? How dumb.

She searched the room for something to cover the window. There were hooks above the glass—drapes had hung there before. Why had they taken them down? Lizzie grabbed the extra blanket and started hanging it on the hooks.

While doing so, she accidentally glanced at the statue and stumbled back in surprise. Helen was staring at her. Her robes swirled, moving around her torso and legs. And the statue was closer—much closer than the night before. Near enough to see that the robes around her were made of water—angry, rushing water.

Lizzie clapped her hands over her eyes. Why did she look? Why?

With her eyes shut, she fumbled around, finding the last loop and hanging the blanket over it. Then she rushed to her bed. "Stop it, Lizzie. Stop it. You're just making everything worse! And if this is a prank, that's just an optical illusion of some sort."

But freaking out was one of her best qualities, and she couldn't push her fears aside. She *had* called Helen. It was the only explanation. There was no way a practical joke could be this detailed.

She must have fallen asleep because sometime later in the night, a muffled thump dragged her from her dreams. In confusion, she rubbed her eyes and looked toward the window where the sound had originated. The blanket had fallen, and clouds now covered the moon.

Just then, lightning struck, followed by a loud thunder crack. Lizzie's skin tingled and she rubbed her arms, trying to get the feeling to go away. A quick procession of lightning bolts flashed across the sky, and the thunder followed so loud that her ears rang. She reached up to turn on the bedside lamp, but it didn't work.

There was a soft knock at the door. "Lizzie?"

Lizzie jumped out of bed and opened to Steph, who was holding candles. "I didn't think you'd be able to sleep with all the thunder. The power's gone out. Take these in case you want light."

Lizzie thanked her and put a couple of candles on the dresser and two big ones on the bedside table. Sudden gratitude that she was a Fire Arete flooded over her—she'd have no problem starting a flame, with or without matches.

After making sure the room was empty, she huddled in bed, trying not to look at the window but unable to help doing so every time the lighting flashed. It was so vivid!

And then one bright blaze revealed something that made her shriek.

The statue was right outside the window, robes of rushing water whirling around it, unseeing stone eyes boring into the room, a hand beckoning for Lizzie to come.

She jerked the blankets over her head, holding

still, praying that someone heard her squeal, that they'd come help her.

Water rushed against the window harder and harder and louder and louder. Something solid rapped on the glass several times, but she ignored it. Lizzie, unable to control the shivers that tore through her body, clung to her legs, knees at her chest, burying her face in the blankets. The wind blew so strongly, it sounded like the house was about to fall apart.

And then there was sudden silence.

Lizzie held her breath, waiting, ears straining. After at least ten agonizing minutes, she pulled a corner of the blanket from her face and peered at the window.

It was empty, the statue gone.

The moon was out again and she dropped the blanket the rest of the way, hoping that maybe— *maybe*—Helen had given up.

Lizzie sat motionless in bed, afraid to do anything but stare at the window. A corner of her brain itched to light a candle. She ignored it at first, then decided the warm light would only help.

Her joints almost frozen from lack of movement, she gathered all the candles from both the bedroom and bathroom—even the decorative ones—and dropped them on the comforter.

One by one, she lit them with her magic, miming the pencil and paper, and placed them throughout the room. Her shaking wasn't too difficult to control and she almost fooled herself into believing she wasn't scared.

Soon, the area was almost as bright as it was when

the actual lights were on. The unique and comforting scent of her magical fire drifted across her nose—like the smell of a match, only stronger, more sulfuric, and without the accompanying burning wood.

Lizzie sat on the bed, staring at the bright candles on the dresser. Her heart and breathing returned to normal and she closed her eyes for a moment, allowing the kinks and fear in her brain to melt away. The morning couldn't come soon enough!

A slight, moist breeze drifted across her face and she opened her eyes, trying to find the source. Nothing was there, but one of the candles on the dresser went out. She frowned, staring at it. "Must be cheap," she whispered, standing to re-light it.

She returned to the bed, preparing to get between the sheets. The candle died again. She rolled her eyes in exasperation, deciding to leave it alone. "Dumb thing." Just as she was sliding her feet under the covers, another candle on the dresser went out. And then another.

She cocked her head, then shivered when the moist breeze blew by again. All the candles in the room flickered, several more dying.

Lizzie jumped from the bed, not wanting to be alone in the dark, and started lighting the candles. She began with the ones on the dresser, then dashed for the others placed throughout the room, burning her hand several times on hot wax. By the time she'd reached those on the bedside table, though, several of the first had died.

Panicked, Lizzie raced from flame to flame, trying to protect them from the breeze that continued to stir the air. She still couldn't see the source—her door was shut and the window wasn't made to open.

Then all the candles went out at the same time.

Oh, no, oh, no! Plunged in darkness, Lizzie whimpered, trying to concentrate enough to create a flame in her hand. Her spark refused to ignite, however. Why now? It always worked for her!

During her rush to light candles, Lizzie had ended up by the window. Unable to stop herself, and using the moonlight, she instinctively looked for the statue. Her shoulders slumped in relief when she saw that it wasn't at the window. The ordeal was over. Helen would leave her alone!

A noise caught her attention. A soft sigh, coming from the other side of the room.

She turned from the window, trying to see in the dark. It was her imagination again. Right?

Then the sound of shifting sheets directed her attention to the other bed. Lizzie put a hand on her chest, clutching her pajama top. She couldn't be sure, but it looked like something—or someone—was under the blankets.

A droplet of water splatted on the wooden floor and Lizzie jumped, backing against the window.

The form under the comforter shifted, groaned, then moved again.

Lizzie's arms and legs froze, her body unwilling to run as she watched a slender hand reach up to rearrange the pillow, making visible a mop of long blond hair on a woman who faced the other direction.

Then the woman rolled over. Lizzie gasped—it was Helen, easily recognizable from her vision of the other day. Not possible. Not possible at all!

Helen's eyes were shut. Was she sleeping?

Lizzie looked at the door, then at the guest bed, then back to the door again. Twenty feet of wood floor separated her from her only escape. Why did the bedroom have to be so large? Could she make it? She had to!

Gathering as much courage as she could, she took a step toward the exit, watching the bed.

The woman's eyes popped open. She stared at Lizzie.

A smile crossed Helen's face and she reached a hand out from under the blanket. "Sutherland, my love. You called for me. You finally called . . ." She closed her eyes, the smile lingering. Then she looked at Lizzie again and shifted the blankets away from her body, revealing robes of water swirling around her. Little streams fell over the side of the bed, puddling on the floor.

Lizzie froze again. She'd never before encountered an Arete as powerful as Helen. What could Lizzie do? Run? Scream? Reason with the woman?

Helen sat up. "I'm ready to take you home." She held out her hand again. "Come along, darling."

Lizzie decided to try reasoning. No way was she going with the statue woman! "Listen, Helen," she said. "I'm not Sutherland. My name is Lizzie. I'm an eighteen-year-old girl, not the man you love. Please, please, leave me alone."

Helen didn't respond. She stared at Lizzie with dark eyes, then stood.

A stronger breeze flowed through the room,

accompanied by something Lizzie rarely felt when away from Katon University—a magical vibration. The power flowing from the woman was unmistakable. Lizzie had no chance against her.

Helen took a step toward Lizzie, both hands now reaching, beckoning. Her hair drifted in the wind, tousling at her shoulders. If this had been a movie, Lizzie would've enjoyed the scene—Helen was freakishly beautiful, her passion and desire for Sutherland romantic. But Lizzie wasn't watching a movie. This was real.

Lizzie backed up against the window and screamed when a bolt of lightning flickered around the woman. She grasped around, trying to find something to throw, then remembered the blanket on the floor and picked it up. She chucked it at Helen, but it went straight through the woman.

"Please don't fight, my dear. We belong together."

Hoping that Helen would be too insubstantial to grab a physical person, Lizzie tried to rush around her. But Helen reached out and grabbed Lizzie's arm with a stone-like grasp. Lizzie screamed again. "Help! Someone!"

Just then, the door to the bedroom burst open. Helen looked back and shrieked at Steph and John. The air crackled around her, and Lizzie felt an electrical current flood through her body, zapping her as it entered the floor below, making her hair stand on end.

"Release the girl," John yelled, holding a golf club.

"You can't keep us apart!" Helen shrieked, pulling Lizzie in closer.

John raised the club and advanced on Helen, but lightning flashed in the room, connecting with the fixture on the ceiling. Bright light burst from the electrical sockets and the bulbs popped, shattering glass everywhere. One strand of electricity shot from Helen's shoulder and struck John, knocking him backward, the club flying from his hands.

Oh, no! Was he okay? Lizzie tried to push away from Helen, but couldn't get out of the woman's grasp.

Steph screamed, running for her husband. She spun around, seemingly unsure what to do. "Lizzie?" Steph yelled. "Are you all right?"

"She won't let go of me." Lizzie squirmed, trying to pry the fingers off her arm. She suddenly remembered the whistle and yelled out, "You've got to destroy the whistle! Smash it! Do something!"

Helen turned back to Lizzie, her eyes glowing with electricity. She opened her mouth and roared, firebolts flowing between her teeth.

Lizzie screamed, but her cry was cut off when something closed around her throat. She gasped and struggled against Helen, realizing the woman was going to kill her. Lizzie clawed at her neck with the other hand—there wasn't anything there. Panic overwhelmed her and she kicked, scratched, did everything she could to get away. Nothing worked.

"We'll live together forever, Sutherland," Helen said. Her expression was peaceful, all traces of anger gone.

Helen's robes swirled around the two women, pulling them together. Lizzie's lungs burned, but she still fought. Then the room started fading away. She was going to die.

A loud crack raked the air.

Helen whirled and shrieked, letting go of Lizzie. The grip on Lizzie's throat released and air rushed back into her lungs. She fell to the floor, clutching her neck. Helen took a step toward Steph, raising her hand. She stumbled. Her watery robes expanded to fill the entire room and began spinning around and around, drenching everything in their path, the wind tearing at Lizzie. Water droplets pelted Lizzie like hail, and she raised her arms to protect herself. She couldn't believe how powerful Helen was—she had so much control!

With the sound of a hurricane and one last bolt of lightning, Helen became stone again and exploded, rock pummeling the entire room. Water splashed up against the walls, then fell. Steph was crouched over her husband, a fire extinguisher—probably the only heavy thing she could find—and the smashed remains of Lizzie's whistle on the floor nearby.

Footsteps sounded in the hall outside and several members of the Smith family rushed into the room.

"Whoa," one of the older daughters said. "What happened here?"

"We had an unexpected visit from . . . uh . . . your father's statue," Steph said, holding John. "She tried to take Lizzie away."

"Are you serious? No way. You're joking, right?"

"Everything will be explained later." Steph got to her knees. "For now, we need to get an ambulance out here to make sure Dad is okay. He got struck by lightning."

Ignoring the expressions of disbelief, Steph began delivering orders and pretty soon, the entire household was awake. People came in and out of the room, carrying buckets and towels and mops. Steph helped Lizzie up, and together, they surveyed the room.

"I guess I shouldn't have spent so much time

decorating last month."

Lizzie smiled, too tired to respond.

An hour later—the Smith cabin was far from the nearest city—the paramedics arrived and took John to the hospital. Steph insisted that Lizzie be checked out as well, and Lizzie didn't argue. It hurt too much to talk.

After a couple of hours, she and John were released, neither having been badly injured.

Nicole was waiting at the cabin. She'd left the moment Lizzie texted her about the trip to the hospital, and had arrived in two hours instead of three.

"Nate and Austin will be coming later today," she said, hugging Lizzie hard.

Lizzie couldn't respond at first. Tears sprang to her eyes. "I'm so glad you're here."

"Me too."

When Steph suggested the girls move into a different room, both agreed. Especially after they learned all the other rooms had curtains.

Andrea Pearson, author of the Mosaic Chronicles, the Kilenya series, and a Utah native, spends as much time writing as possible. When not doing that, she can be found hiking, biking, or watching a good movie with her husband. She graduated from Brigham Young University with a BS in Communication Disorders, and she loves art and music.

To learn more about Andrea, visit her website at www.andreapearsonbooks.com

Bonus chapter from *Perceive, Mosaic Chronicles Book Three*:

CHAPTER ONE

℘ ✦ ℃

Nicole's body ached from sitting in the same position for several hours. She'd never liked long car rides, and though this was nowhere near the longest she'd experienced, it still made her antsy and cranky. She couldn't wait to get out and stretch her legs.

At least the company had been good—her best friend, Lizzie, sat next to her on the backseat. Professor Coolidge was driving, with Austin, one of the best-looking guys she'd ever met, sitting up front with him. The two had conversed more with each other than they had with the girls, but every now and then, their conversation spilled over, and Nicole had the opportunity to learn something new about the world she'd grown up in.

Nicole was an Arete—the fourth child born to her parents—and as such, she had magical abilities. All Fourths did. Because she had naturally blond hair, her powers originated from the element Wind, but she'd only been able to Channel her abilities a few times.

Lizzie was a redhead and could manipulate Fire to

a degree. Austin and Coolidge were both dark-headed and controlled Earth. Because most of the people on the planet had dark hair of some shade or another—Asians, blacks, Middle Easterners, and such—their abilities were a little more common than Lizzie's and Nicole's. This created a lot more competition for them, forcing the more powerful to branch into Wind and Fire and sometimes even Water, which was represented by dirty blond or light brown hair and was the second most-common ability.

That was what the men were discussing up front while Nicole stared out the window, wishing their trip to Moses Lake, Washington would hurry up and end. They'd been in the car for two-and-a-half hours.

She turned her thoughts from the conversation and let them stray to the manor on the far side of Moses Lake they would be visiting, and the old man who owned it. Coolidge had been quiet about the reason they were heading there, though he had let on that it would hugely impact Nicole's ability to Channel. She figured it had to do with her focus—the cello—which meant Coolidge had most likely gotten his hands on one.

Nicole sighed. She'd found a cello in Ohio that helped her Channel, but it—and the woman who owned it—had disappeared while she'd been studying there for three weeks.

"Nicole," Coolidge said, "I've already told you this trade was difficult to arrange, and Austin says you've guessed that it's a cello. Well, Albert wants to see you play it before he'll allow you to take it back with us. Just . . . be careful with this instrument, okay? He's very attached to it."

"Of course."

Soon, they were driving through the streets of Moses Lake, then turning onto and following Wheeler Road. Nicole watched as acres and acres of farmland passed on either side of them. After twenty minutes, the landscape began to be dotted with trees.

"We're not far now," Coolidge said, peering into the distance.

Nicole watched as the trees turned into a heavy forest. It somehow seemed unnatural, though she couldn't put her finger on why. A foreign feeling accompanied the massive, twisted trees that towered over the car and cast them all into dark shadows.

Coolidge slowed, then turned onto a newly paved road. They pulled up to a large, ornate gate and he rolled down the window and punched in a code. The gates opened, admitting entrance, and the car continued onward.

Five minutes after passing through the gates, Nicole caught glimpses of the manor, but it wasn't until they entered a huge clearing that she saw everything in full. Her jaw dropped.

She had grown up in a wealthy family with a large estate, but her house had nothing on this place. Turrets and towers pierced the sky. Gables and heavy beams seemed to go for a mile at least. The place must have been tens of thousands of square feet. It was large enough to house a village.

Dead vines crawled up most of the walls—Nicole guessed that if it had been summer, the vines would be green and lush. But at the beginning of November, they only made the place look dead and creepy.

"Brings to mind *Rose Red*, doesn't it?" Coolidge asked.

Austin and Nicole nodded. That about summed up Nicole's feelings.

Lizzie hissed to Nicole, "What's *Rose Red*?"

"Stephen King," Nicole said. "You wouldn't like it."

"Well, I think this place is beautiful." Lizzie sighed. "And romantic."

Coolidge chuckled. "Don't read or watch *Rose Red*, and you can keep that opinion."

An older man—probably Albert—waited on the porch, a serene smile on his face, arms behind his back. He wore a Mr. Rogers sweater—the red, zip-up type—and faded slacks.

Coolidge pulled the car to a stop, and the four of them exited, Nicole stretching her back, getting out a few pops.

Albert approached Coolidge, and they shook hands and hugged. Nicole watched Albert closely, waiting for him to exhibit characteristics of someone who lived in a creepy old manor, but the man was kind, gentle, and warm.

He invited them inside, and Nicole was surprised to find that the interior of the house was incredibly clean. No dust or cobwebs anywhere. It was in pristine condition. She smiled. Her mom would approve.

The house had been upgraded a few times since having been built, and modern light fixtures graced the walls and ceilings. Albert kept the place well lit, and Nicole appreciated that.

After passing several halls and rooms and taking many turns, they entered a room that had stringed instrument corpses and parts hanging on the walls—bridges, scrolls, necks, and other sections, along with whole instruments. It had never occurred to Nicole that instruments could be creepy, but here they were.

"I'm surprised your car made it this far," Albert said after they'd all been seated on worn, but clean brown couches.

Coolidge frowned. "Why?"

"Ever since the meteor hit, machines haven't been working very well in this area. We're fine in here, but cars have completely stalled in parts of the driveway."

Coolidge raised his eyebrows. "I haven't heard anything about a meteor. How big was it?"

"Five feet across. And it didn't really fall from the sky, which is probably why you haven't heard anything. It just sort of exploded into the middle of my property, right next to the home of a man who's been employed by my family for years. We had people come out and test the metal, and the only conclusive thing they came up with is that it wasn't from earth. But the fact that it didn't fall from the sky says it has to be." He leaned back in his seat. "It's a complete mystery."

"I'd like to see it," Coolidge said. "And I'm sure my students would as well."

Nicole, Austin, and Lizzie all nodded.

"Can't. It's gone now."

Nicole frowned. Gone? Too bad. It would have been awesome to see.

"How?" Coolidge asked. "Taken away by the 'authorities'?"

"Nope," Albert said. "We had a severe rainstorm a few days ago. The meteor was struck multiple times by lightning, then disappeared completely."

No one said anything for a moment, then finally, Albert turned to Austin. "Professor Coolidge has told me about you. You're quite accomplished."

Austin glanced at him briefly and nodded, then stared at a spot above Albert's head. Nicole smiled to herself. She knew Austin well enough to recognize that he wasn't enjoying the attention, especially from someone he wasn't familiar with. She ached to join him on his couch and rub his hand, helping him get out of himself, but she resisted. The last time they'd talked, while flying home from Arches National Park, she'd gotten the impression that yes, he was interested in her, but that he was struggling with knowing whether to date her or to get back with his ex-girlfriend, Savannah.

That didn't make it easier to control her impulse, though. And for the first time in a while, she let her eyes explore his features, enjoying the curves and angles—the perfection—of his face.

"How many of the four main elements can you control now?" Albert asked him.

Austin glanced at him, then away. "All but one—Wind."

"Makes sense. You shouldn't be far off from that one, though."

Nicole had recently learned that Arete abilities formed a sort of cycle, with the ability just above each Arete being the easiest to learn, while the one directly below was hardest. Earth, Water, Fire, Wind. Austin, as an Earth Arete, was struggling to learn Wind, but had quickly grasped Water. Nicole would learn the elements gradually too—Wind, Earth, Water, then finally, Fire, if she stuck with it. Which she planned on doing.

"How do you like looking after the house on your own?" Coolidge asked after another moment of silence.

Albert shrugged. "It's nothing—I'm used to doing most everything by myself anyway. It saves a great deal of money."

Lizzie frowned. "But you're a billionaire—Coolidge said so. Why do you need to save money?"

Albert's eyes twinkled. "You're a very forthright young lady, Miss Lizzie."

Lizzie looked at her feet. "Sorry, I just . . . I'm just curious."

"Don't be sorry. I don't mind questions." He leaned back in his chair. "People get rich by living within their means and not getting into debt. Yes, I inherited a lot of money and land, but the habits of my parents and grandparents who lived through the Great Depression aren't easily shed, and I've nearly quadrupled my inheritance." He pointed to an old lemonade stand in the corner. "I've had that since I was four and mature enough to understand the concept behind a product in exchange for money. My father built it for me."

His eyes clouded over, and he appeared to be deep in thought. Several silent moments passed, and Nicole met eyes with Lizzie, wondering how or if they should break the silence. It was awkward, like wool fabric against sensitive skin.

"Albert?" Coolidge asked. "Are you all right?"

Albert shook himself. "Yes, I'm fine. I . . . I've

had two Aretes become deathly ill nearly the minute they enter the forest behind the manor. It's presenting a problem, and I'm finding myself frequently distracted." He glanced at the girls. "Lest you think my mind skips around a lot, there was a small connection. My father fell ill with pneumonia and died from complications. I've had a bit of a cold that just doesn't seem to go away. It's pretty much unrelated, but those two Aretes have had me thinking a lot about mortality lately."

He straightened. "Would anyone like a glass of lemonade?"

All four of his visitors said yes, and he jumped to his feet, insisting on doing it himself.

A moment later, when everyone had a glass in his or her hand, Albert glanced at Nicole. "It's time to introduce you to Niko."

"Niko?" Lizzie asked.

"My cello. Named after cellist and composer Nikolaus Kraft."

"You gave your cello a nickname?" Lizzie said. "That's kind of cute."

Albert smiled. "Thank you, Miss Lizzie. I've always striven for 'kind of cute.' Maybe I should have made full cute my goal, but alas, I didn't." He turned to Nicole. "How long have you been playing?"

"Since I was five."

Albert nodded. "Do you enjoy the cello?"

"Oh, yes. Very much."

"Are you any good?"

Nicole felt a flush cross her cheeks, and she glanced at Austin for a moment. He gave her a half smile, warming her insides, and she looked back at Albert.

"Well . . . I . . ." She cleared her throat. "Yes, I believe I have a gift."

Albert nodded. "Before I make any decisions, I'd like to hear you play, if that's all right." He smiled, leaning forward. "But you need to understand something. I've been invited to several private concerts by both Yo-Yo Ma and Bernard Greenhouse."

Nicole wasn't sure how to respond to that. She definitely wasn't as talented as either man, but she wasn't horrible, either. She hoped Albert would approve of her playing. "Um . . . okay."

"Well, I'll get the instrument." Albert stood and left the room.

It didn't take long for him to return. He set the case in front of Nicole, then opened it, showing her the cello. She reached for it, but he shook his head.

"No, I'll do that myself." He undid a strap around the neck, then pulled out the cello, holding it for a moment, hesitating. Obviously, it meant a lot to him.

After looking at it for a while, he finally handed it to Nicole.

The instant the instrument was in Nicole's hands, she felt an electrical charge run through her, lifting her hair, making her feel lighter than air for a moment. A floating sensation from the charge made her limbs raise unbidden. It was accompanied by a rush of warmth that enveloped her.

She smiled, welcoming the feeling, and glanced at the others. "Did anyone sense that?"

Albert leaned back in his seat. "Even I did, and I'm not an Arete. Clearly, the cello calls to you." He motioned to her. "Don't Channel your powers. Just play."

Nicole did so, starting with a selection by Dvorak, then moving on to Camille Saint-Saens. At first, it was easy. The notes seemed to sing and breathe their way out of the cello. But after a moment, Nicole could sense a pull on the magical currents that quietly surrounded her. She felt them flowing toward the ocean of magic that had started to build again after her return from Ohio. She struggled to contain them. To prevent the dam from bursting.

Her mouth popped open, realizing that for the first time, she was pushing her powers away rather than begging them to flow to her. Weird! And wonderful!

She played for several minutes, casually noticing—but pretending *not* to notice—the expressions of those around her. Lizzie was grinning. Coolidge was nodding, a look of pride on his face. Albert's eyes were closed, enjoying the melodies.

And Austin . . . Austin. He watched her closely, enraptured. Their gazes met. Nicole felt a thrill at the intensity of his expression, at the possessiveness there, the pride, the sense of protection she felt in his gaze. Her heart warmed, the heat spreading to her stomach and into her legs and arms. How was it possible that this talented and powerful man was interested in and attracted to her?

After several minutes, Albert motioned for her to stop and took the cello from her. "I don't want you playing unless you are in the presence of at least one other Arete or myself. Never alone—not until you master your powers." He put the cello back into the case, fastening the straps and zipper. "Your professor tells me you exhibit great strengths—that you have abilities waiting to be released. I don't want you damaging my instrument."

"Especially since she already controls wood to an extent," Austin said.

Nicole nodded and gave her word to Albert.

What Austin said was true, and it would be a while before she'd be able to stop reliving the experiences they'd had while in Arches National Park. Nicole had nearly killed herself by forcing her powers to go beyond what she was ready to handle. Wood was under Earth powers, and since she hadn't mastered her own abilities, it was dangerous for her to mess around with Earth.

"How old is this cello?" she asked. The one that belonged to Mrs. Morse in Ohio had been at least a hundred years old—she could sense that while playing. And this cello felt even older than that.

Albert scratched his head, thinking. "Let's see . . . around three hundred years."

Nicole's eyes widened. "How can you be sure?"

"Easy. It's one of sixty remaining Stradivari."

Nicole gasped. "It's ... it's a Stradivarius? Why on *earth* are you letting me touch it, let alone take it home?"

"It's on loan to you for only a week, maybe two. If you don't develop your powers before the time is up, you're welcome to stay here temporarily." He motioned out the window. "My tenant's daughter comes and cleans for me for several hours every day, as payment for letting them continue living on the property, and she would keep you company. Honestly, she could even benefit from . . . well . . . from meeting a girl close to her age who isn't so *sheltered*."

Nicole shrugged. "I'll consider it." She hoped she'd develop her abilities before then, just to prevent the hassle of having to move around so much, but a week or two wasn't a lot of time.

Lizzie frowned. "So, you're letting Nicole borrow a priceless cello. What are we giving you in return?"

"Professor Coolidge has provided me with something of equal importance."

"What could possibly be worth millions of dollars?" Lizzie asked.

Albert shrugged. "Not much that I would need or want. But what I'm getting is worth millions of *hours*. It's an automatic food preserver."

"An automatic food preserver?" Austin asked. "I've never heard of one."

Nicole smiled that it made even Austin speak up— such a rare occurrence.

"That's because only one exists. The family that still lives on my property is sort of Amish. They don't have power or plumbing, and they maintain no connection to the outside world. I allow them to stay as long as they provide me with food. And they do—they grow quite an abundance. I preserve almost all of it myself. It's much cheaper than buying food from a grocery store that's over half an hour of a drive. But, as you probably know, preserving foods the old-fashioned way can be very time-consuming.

"With the automatic food preserver, my life will become much easier. You put the ingredients in one side and the canning containers in another, and the machine does the rest. Boiling, steaming, heating, cleaning, zipping, sealing, everything. Magic is involved, of course, because no machine would be able to do it all."

Nicole shook her head. She had to admit, something like that would be very handy.

Just then, a man with a sparse, graying beard stepped into the doorway. He held a hat in his hands and wore a pair of faded overalls.

"Oh, Winston," Albert said. "Come in and meet my friends."

Winston entered the room, a large grin on his face. He shook hands with everyone as Albert introduced them. He was followed by a teenage girl with brown, sparkly eyes and dark ringlets. She wore a dress that reminded Nicole of a real pioneer. It was obvious by how similar the two looked that she was Winston's daughter.

"Winston and his family are the tenants I was telling you about." Albert motioned the girl forward. "This is Prudy, Winston's oldest daughter. She's the one who comes to clean every day."

Prudy curtsied, her long dress bunching as she dipped. She held a basket full of apples in her hands. A bonnet hung down her back.

Coolidge motioned to Winston. "Albert here was telling us that a meteor struck near your house."

Winston bobbed his head. "Yeah, it did. 'Cept, it didn't struck—it appeared." He pointed to the basket of apples Prudy carried. "That meteor done somethin' good, I tell ya. It gone and made the crops produce in overabundance!" He stepped to his daughter's side and pulled out several apples, then passed them around the room. "My best crop of Granny Smiths this year. And ya'll get the pleasure of bein' the first to try 'em."

Winston blinked, looking at everyone. "Well, go ahead."

Nicole looked down at the apple in her hand. It was beautiful—huge, bright green, luscious. The prettiest Granny Smith she'd ever seen. She rubbed off a spot, then took a bite, noticing the others do the same.

She immediately gagged, spitting the apple flesh out of her mouth, grabbing for her glass of lemonade, nearly knocking it over in her hurry to get it. She wasn't the only one—all the others were gulping down their drinks, trying to remove the awful taste from their mouths. It was repulsive—like rotted worms that had died while eating pizza.

Nicole finished off her glass, but the flavors still burned on her tongue, making her eyes smart. Nothing she did helped.

Winston stood there, horrified, a look of shock on his face. Then he raced around, grabbing the apples from Albert and his visitors. "I'm sorry—so sorry," he said over and over again. He and Prudy rushed from the room, carrying the basket.

They returned moments later with tall glasses of milk, which everyone accepted gratefully.

"I don't know what happened to them apples," Winston said. "They're usually so good."

Nicole downed the glass of milk, noticing that the taste of rot subsided. She leaned back in her chair, breathing deeply, rubbing her face and the tears from her eyes.

Austin coughed. "I don't think I'll have another apple, if that's all right."

Winston chuckled, then apologized again, but Albert stopped him. "It's not your fault—these things happen."

Winston nodded. "I know. I'm still sorry."

Prudy took everyone's now-empty glasses, and she and Winston left, obviously ashamed and embarrassed.

"How humiliating," Nicole said. "They couldn't possibly have known that would happen."

Albert shook his head. "No, they couldn't have."

Wanting to wash her face, Nicole asked where the bathroom was, then excused herself. Following Albert's directions, she passed through several rooms and down a hallway until she found the place. It had obviously once been a closet that was converted sometime after indoor plumbing was invented. The light was dim and the room smelled of old wood.

Nicole washed her face, relishing the feel of cool water, especially after that experience with the apple. She peered at herself in the mirror, noticing that all traces of makeup were now long gone.

"Stupid, disgusting apple," she whispered.

She pulled mascara out of her purse and applied it, then noticed a spider crawling along the sink. "Oh, great," she whispered, then glanced in the mirror, looking behind herself. The bathroom was still empty.

"I know you're here," Nicole said. "Just . . . just come out."

A faint white outline appeared next to her, then strengthened in substance until the old woman Nicole knew to expect after seeing spiders stood next to her.

Nicole frowned. "I thought we had an agreement that I wouldn't read the book until I'm ready to." Nicole knew that wasn't exactly the promise she'd made while in Arches, but she hoped the old woman wouldn't remember.

"You *must* read it, Nicole."

Nicole jumped, hand on her heart. "You can talk? Since when can you talk?"

The old woman shook her head, her long gray hair billowing around her. "Read the book."

Nicole sighed in exasperation. "I'll think about it." She put her mascara in her purse and left the bathroom, heading through the manor to the instrument room.

"It's time to go," Coolidge said. He pulled a business card from his pocket and handed it to Albert. "You've already got my cell, but I'd like to get frequent updates on the situation with the meteor." He pointed to the card. "That the number to my office, where I spend a lot of time. My cell doesn't work there. Feel free to call me if you ever need help."

Albert agreed to do so, then escorted the four out to Coolidge's car, where he helped Austin and Coolidge remove his new contraption from the trunk. Once the food preserver was set up in the manor and the space was clear, Albert brought out the cello and gently placed it in the trunk, tucking blankets around the case to keep it from sliding.

When he'd finished, he glanced up at Nicole. "There are obviously much better ways to transport a cello of this worth. But seeing as how most cars can't make it to the manor, this will have to do."

Nicole was quiet the whole way home, thinking about the cello and the old woman. She didn't look forward to being in the same room with that book again—the one the woman wanted her to read. At the start of school a couple of months earlier, she'd touched it and had awakened it, then for several weeks, it, and the creepy shadow that dwelled in it, had followed her everywhere. Coolidge had locked it away in a magical cabinet in his office, where it waited, gaining strength, calling to her.

Now that Nicole knew how to Channel and would be developing her powers, the time to read the book was upon her. She only hoped she'd be ready for whatever happened.

Made in the USA
Monee, IL
04 April 2021